STITCHED LIPS

STITCHED LIPS

An Anthology of Horror from Silenced Voices

KEN MACGREGOR

Dragon's Roost Press

Dragon's Roost Press

thedragonsroost.biz

TABLE OF CONTENTS

INTRODUCTION

Jim McLeod

You are probably sitting there, scratching your head, wondering why on earth this man, of all people, is writing the introduction to an anthology designed to promote voices which are, at best, historically ignored—or at worst, silenced. A privileged white male is not the sort of person who should be here with his soliloquy about representation in the horror genre.

You are probably correct in that assumption—but bear with me: I might not change your mind, but I might just put the case forward for my presence in this anthology.

Take a seat, and buckle up—this will get very personal, and it might even lose me some friends, but, hopefully, it will change your opinion of me one way or another.

This year (2021) will mark the thirteenth year of Ginger Nuts of Horror. Since its inception, I like to think that we have evolved: from being something to do to keep me out of trouble into a healthy and positive voice in the horror community. A voice that has always strived to represent authors from all walks of life. It was never a conscious decision to have the site as a voice for everyone; it was more the result of organic growth, from picking up new members of the Ginger Nuts family. I'd like to think that we have a very diverse family, with each member adding their voice to the website's existence.

However—and this is where it will get raw—if I were still the person I was thirty-odd years ago, the site would be a different beast altogether.

You see, the pre-university, eighteen-year-old man-child that was me was a very different person. I'm not going to try and make excuses for myself, like every apologist who gets caught out does, but let me try and put it into context.

I grew up in a small town with the eighties being my teenage years, and it was an insular time and place; everyone I knew looked like and acted as I did. I had no exposure to anything that wasn't a straight white male or female. And I am disgusted to say I was a bit of a racist homophobe. I was never vocal about my views—not that that makes it any better; the thoughts were still in my head, and they would have presented themselves outwardly with at least some sort of subconscious act. I would best describe it as being suspicious and wary of those perceived as gay or having a different skin colour. Hell, I even used the P-word [P*ki – a racial slur directed at people of South Asian descent – editor] when popping out to the corner shop. I'm not proud of that, and this might sound flippant, but were I ever allowed to travel back in time to meet myself, I would punch myself in the face and give myself a stern talking to.

In those days, my attitude came purely from a place of ignorance and isolation from people who weren't carbon copies of me. When I went to university, I grew, and started the journey of change into the person I am today.

At university, I met people from all walks of life. As I became friends with more and more diverse people, my attitudes changed. I realised that things like skin colour, sexuality, race, religion, or disabilities were not things that I should judge people on. Those things, while they define the individual, do not define their worth, relevance, or their right to be heard and represented as equals.

Those old attitudes of mine were not only harmful, dangerous, and despicable, they prevented me from experiencing things that would only bring me joy. In the four years of being a student, I went from brutish oaf to active ally of such things as the LGBTQ society the Society of Black Students.

I am not that man anymore. To paraphrase the songwriter Jason Isbell, "There's a man who walks beside me. It is who I used to be, and I wonder if you see him and confuse him with me." The teenage me is still there; he always will be; I can't change my past; he sits there on my shoulder each day to remind me of the man I am now. I will carry the shame of who I was with me to the grave.

After that long-winded monologue about myself, it is time to put that into the context of this anthology. Even though it is now 2021, the horror genre has always been a world dominated by straight white men. There have been massive headways made in terms of diversification, but, for the main, it is the same old names, the same old points of view being pushed forward by the presses, the reviewers, and the genre's fans. When we still have to have things like Women in Horror Month or Black Horror Month, that should tell you that the genre needs to pull itself out of the old ways and embrace a more diverse way of doing things.

You are reading this anthology introduction; I shall assume that you are a horror fan. You will understand that horror isn't just about monsters. It is a genre that has the power to tackle some of the most challenging topics of human existence. But if all you read are the same old experiences from the same old point of view, you'll be missing out on some of the most rewarding examples of horror out there.

There is a rich vein of talent out there from authors who are sadly silenced by the masses' never-ending chatter. And that cannot be a good thing, for so many reasons. Even if you don't feel the need to read horror from a diverse set of voices, there *are* those who do, who need and want to read from a richer font. There's no such thing as someone else's fight for representation. Your experiences and voices aren't the only things worth fighting for. I could spend this section listing all of the great authors you should be reading, but I will invariably miss out on someone I should have mentioned. And you know what? It's not that difficult to discover new writers: check out sites like mine, and places like SciFi and Scary Reviews, Ladies of Horror Fiction, Diversity in Horror, or even do a quick keyword search on Twitter. There are loads of outlets doing great things to lift the voices of others out there.

As a species, we are, in simplistic terms, tribalistic: we gravitate to others like us, with a Venn diagram of interactions with others who are less like us. But what if your primary circle of the Venn diagram doesn't exist?

Where do you fit in? There are countless fans of horror out there who don't know where to look for the books and films that speak to them. We all want to feel as though we belong somewhere— it's human nature, we all want to share in the experiences of those we feel companionship with, but it can be challenging to seek them out. Reading and sharing your love for a book on social media has the power to create new friendships and new bonds amongst people who get you, who understand you're not just your struggles, but the things that make your world view *yours*. As a species, we can never move forward and realise our full potential until we can have a society where we are all treated as equals.

This is why websites like mine have a duty to use their influence to lift up the voices of those who are woefully underrepresented. Without meaning to sound arrogant, Ginger Nuts of Horror has one of the loudest voices out there, and we would be negligent not to use our voice to lift others. But how do we do that? There is no easy answer, I certainly don't have a fix-it-all solution, but speaking from my own experiences, hitting people over the head, or screaming in their faces that they need to change, never works.

People don't like to be browbeaten; they dig their heels in and become even more belligerent. From a personal perspective, I think the answer is to change them by immersing them in stories from authors they would never usually read. That can only happen if people like myself— with loud voices— review, promote, and talk about authors from all walks of life. Just think: there could be that one person struggling with who they are, and someone recommends that one book that speaks to them and makes them feel they aren't alone in feeling the way they do, and reading that book brings them back from the brink. Art has that power, and it has certainly done this for me on numerous occasions.

But, Jim, if we are continually pushing diverse authors, what about us poor straight white male authors, when do we get our month? Isn't this a form of reverse equality and cancel culture? Some of you might think that's a joke; I dare you to take a look through social media on the first day or two of any month looking to promote diversity and inclusion. It's funny how questions like this only ever come from those in a place of privilege, like straight white male authors (and, to a lesser extent, straight white female authors). I get it: you want to have your stories read; it's the driving force of being an author. But *every* author deserves that, and as a white author, you have so many more doors open to you, and so few doors ever shut in your face. If every author believed that all other authors aren't competition, and we all worked together, everyone who reads horror would have a much more enriched and rewarding time.

I want to end on a positive note, having been on this side of the genre for close to thirteen years, I have seen a quantum shift in the dynamics of the genre, we are heading in the right direction; it may still be too slow or not diverse enough for some, however, despite my grumpy online persona, I am optimistic. I firmly believe that we will get there, there are more of us than them, and if we all help to unstitch the stitches keeping the mouths of the underrepresented shut, and boost their voices, we can turn this into a roar to shake the heavens.

THE WORDEATERS

R.L. Meza

I wake in the gloom of our one-bedroom trailer, struggling to make sense of the shadow standing in the corner, and it is my first instinct that almost kills us. I whisper—say, "Momma"—as I reach to her side of the twin bed and shake her. Eyes snap open at the sound of my voice, but they are not my mother's eyes. Moonlight slants sideways through the small window, and the eyes in the corner gleam, wet and unblinking. Numerous. I am twelve, too old to be afraid of the dark and certain that I am having a nightmare. Still, I shake my mother harder and say, "Momma, wake up. There's something in the corner—"

The words catch in my throat, as the shape in the shadows begins to writhe. It boils, expands, until the eye-studded mass of its head is bent below the ceiling, the bulk of its body obscuring half of the window. Weak moonlight plays over the ruinous landscape of its mottled, rippling flesh. Beside me, my mother groans. Yawns. With half of the window's light blocked by shadow, only the whites of Momma are visible—the glint of her teeth, the stuttering flash of her corneas as she blinks away sleep. I force my aching hands to release their hold on the brass bed frame, but they are pale, drugged birds flapping through the darkness, flying too slow to cover her mouth.

"Agatha? What's—"

Bubbling skin and twitching muscle eclipse all but the upper corner of the bedroom window. Above the foot of our bed, the ceiling is a night sky of glittering eyes. Momma's scream is muffled by my hands, reduced to a warm blast of heat that hisses between my clamped fingers. Her eyes bulge and roll towards me, questioning. Unable to remove my hands, terrified of feeding the growing shape in the corner, I lean over her, frantic to make her understand. I shake my head vigorously, tangled brown curls whipping my cheeks, and hope that my message will translate in the featureless dim.

Momma's fingers fall away from my wrists. She nods. I allow one of my hands to stray from her mouth to point, trembling, at the corner. Pressing my finger to my lips, I wait until she nods again, then remove my other hand. Warm arms enfold me, and Momma draws me to her chest, kisses my forehead. Her heart thuds against my cheek, matching my own racing heartbeat. I picture them together, pounding forward like stampeding horses with frothing mouths and wolf-torn flanks.

My lungs grow tight. A weight settles on my chest, and I panic, thinking that the shape in the corner has finally reached the bed, crawled on top of me to crush the air from my lungs. Momma grabs me by the chin, forces me to look at her and brings her curled, empty hand up to her mouth. I wheeze. My throat is a choked straw, the air unbreathable mud. It takes all my concentration to interpret the squeeze of her thumb and two fingers.

The inhaler—*my* inhaler—is in our tiny bathroom across the hall. The door to the hallway is closed, painted with a triangle of light no larger than Momma's hand. Finger-like projections tickle the triangle's edge, wavering like black kelp in an invisible current. I'm wondering whether the door will open with that bulk of shadow stuffed behind it, when the red digital numbers of Momma's alarm clock shift to 6:00 am, and classical music erupts from the speakers. Momma stiffens with a sharp gasp.

The shape hunched over the foot of our bed, lurking between the window and our door to freedom, does not move. I feel Momma's hand pressing into the small of my back, urging me towards the bedroom door, and my foot touches down on the threadbare carpet to a chorus of string instruments. Playful, lilting, the music is an accompaniment deserving of an animated princess, dancing through the forest with a host of smiling animals. But I am a wretch, tiptoeing across the bedroom, exaggerated movements a poor imitation of stealth. Glancing over my shoulder, I see Momma lowering her feet to the floor. The doorknob is cold in my palm. I twist.

I inch the door open, until I feel resistance from the shape behind it. The gap is wide enough for me to slip through, but I hesitate—my hand still holding the knob on Momma's side of the door—unwilling to separate from our shared space. Momma is only three steps from the door to the hallway, when the classical music cuts off.

"GOOOD MOOORNING, CALIFORNIA. YOU ARE LISTENING TO 'THE WAKE-UP CALL' WITH TY WEST, ONLY ON KWYP-FM. THAT WAS BEETHOVEN'S 'SYMPHONY NO. 5 IN—"

The shape behind the door blooms outward, all branching limbs, roiling muscle, and cascading fat. Beneath the ragged sound of Momma's screaming, Ty West rambles on, but the noise is muffled by the closed door. I blink, confused, at the place below my left wrist, where my hand has vanished between the door and its frame. Agony blossoms, my vision swims, and still I am unable to breathe, pinned across the hallway from the bathroom. In the glow of the night light beside the sink, the inhaler sits on the counter.

I wrench the doorknob with my right hand and slam my weight against the door. Vibrations thrum through the barrier. Momma is no longer screaming, and I wish that Ty West would stop talking—would shut up, *just shut up and play the music.* Violins. A cello. Flutes. I throw myself into the door, bruising my shoulder, and my left hand slides free—a blood-slicked glove filled with broken bones. Stumbling across the hall, I trip on the threshold of the bathroom and sag against the counter; I clutch the edge of the sink and drag myself upright. With a soft hiss, the inhaler loosens the iron bands around my chest. Another puff, and I'm able to sob.

I allow myself six long, deep breaths to think, while I pull the hand towel from the metal ring above the sink and wrap it around my ruined hand. Gritting my teeth, I wind first aid tape around the makeshift bandage to secure it, then stuff the inhaler into the pocket of my sweatpants. I hurry down the hall to the kitchen table, where I fumble with a notepad and pen, scrawling a quick message across the lined yellow paper: *Momma, u ok?*

My feet whisper over the carpet. I kneel and peek through the crack below the bedroom door, listening for Momma. Clarinets. Trombones. I've folded my note in half, prepared to slip it under the door with the pen, but I pause and shake my head. If the shape in the corner has covered the window, it will be too dark for Momma to see. With a grimace, I force my right hand to the door and knock. Double basses. A tuba. The paper slides a third of the way under the door and stops, wrinkling beneath my fingertips. I withdraw the note, stained and trailing ichor. In the glow of the bathroom night light, I squint at the fluid blurring the ink and hear muffled trumpets give way to Ty West. The bedroom door explodes outward, raining splinters into my hair. As Ty West delivers the morning weather, the growing mass expands into the hall, and there is just time for me to slam the bathroom door closed behind me before it begins thumping the door and walls with the hectic rhythm of a kraken trapped in a bass drum. With a sharp *crack*, the bathroom door bows inward.

I climb onto the toilet, slip. Bang my knee against the tank with a strangled yelp. My toes are slick with the fluid leaking across the linoleum. They're tingling, going numb. The dingy pink drapes are knotted in my fist, torn away to expose the narrow window above the toilet. I fumble with the lock. The window jogs aside an inch, then wedges at an angle in the frame. It has always done this—a problem for Momma to fix, with patient jostling. Perhaps it is the stuck window that summons her back from that writhing darkness, because suddenly I can hear Momma's voice at the door, and I'm spilling from the toilet to greet her.

Maybe I've struck my head and forgotten. Or it's the pain—the shock. It's Momma's voice outside the door, but I don't recognize the words tumbling through the cracked wood, and she won't pause for breath to give me a chance to catch on. Sounds, so many sounds, the words buried deep within. Prehistoric beasts drowning in tar. I whisper, "Momma?"

A low, wet chortle, and the door is a splintered maw, opening wide to swallow me. I picture words bubbling up from the muck-filled pit of Momma's throat, can almost hear the popping sounds of vowels surfacing on her tongue, consonants worming between her lips, hideous and misshapen. Bach comes to my rescue. The organ's melancholic notes drift through the fresh silence in the trailer, unpolluted by voices. I wonder if Ty West is aware of the plight he's put me in—whether he's chosen this piece as a mockery or a parting gift—but there's no time to wait for "Sweet Death" to find me. Back to the window.

I wrestle the lid from the toilet tank, my skinny arms quaking beneath its weight. It's difficult to grip the porcelain with my hand swaddled in the towel, but I ignore the blinding pain and heave the lid up, over my head. I drive the slab forward, slamming it into the window with all my strength. Cracks arch through the glass. I force the lid up again, hissing through my teeth with the effort. I strike, and the frame buckles. Glass shatters. A third blow, and the window is now a hole, the screen lying on the gravel below.

Using my towel-wrapped hand to knock away the remaining shards of glass, I press my arms together on either side of my head, as though I'm preparing to dive, and try to wiggle through the window. My shoulders catch. The window's frame digs into my chest, and I feel a stab of panic at the sound of Ty-*fucking*-West at my heels. He's announcing a commercial break. I force my lungs to exhale and squirm forward into the cold morning air. Behind me, the trailer sounds as though it's being slowly fed into a garbage disposal. Metal squeals, wood snaps, as the growing mass gorges itself on cheerful, long-winded advertisements and surges into the bathroom. I feel the clammy press of its flesh against the soles of my feet, and then human fingers close around my ankle.

Momma is dragging me backwards and spewing garbled phrases, while a cheerful jingle assures me that Pete's Septic Service is "number one in the number two business," and my hands scrabble at the outer wall of the—the what? My mind gropes for a word that isn't there. Momma's chattering, digging her—an image flashes in my mind: hard, sharp tips gouging the skin of my ankle, the tips of Momma's fingers —*fingernails!* She's digging her nails in. It hurts, and her blathering is rising in volume. Momma's reeling me back into the bathroom, screaming phrases that are impossible to ignore. I picture them leaking across the folds of my brain like spilled ink, blotting out meaning, reducing words to vague shapes without color.

CHORUS OF WHISPERS

Sarah Hans

Orphelia's procedure took place on a sunny Monday afternoon. She and her mother arrived early and stood in line outside the surgery with other mothers and daughters, waiting their turn, the temperature gradually rising until Orphelia's clothes grew scratchy and hot, and her skin tender to the touch.

Eventually they made it into the shade of the waiting room. Orphelia's stomach growled but she didn't complain about her hunger; Mummy had already told her she wasn't allowed to eat before the procedure. She watched as other girls her age were dragged from the surgical suite by weeping mothers. Some of the girls walked stiff-legged, with wide eyes and ashen faces. Others clutched at their mothers and wept soundlessly.

Orphelia's legs quivered and she wanted to run from the room. Her mother's huge, sweaty hand gripped her tiny one. When it was her turn, Orphelia's mother signed various papers and the nurse stamped them. Mummy folded up and tucked them into the pocket of her voluminous skirt.

They went into the surgical suite. There was a tall doctor in a white coat, a big chair with straps on the arms. An injection made the world go fuzzy and gray. When she roused, moments later, her throat was on fire. She wanted to scream but air passing over her savaged larynx was agony. The pain was so severe the world tilted sideways when she tried to sit up. Mummy offered her a hand and Orphelia slid obediently from the chair. Her legs wobbled under her and Mummy gave her a moment to get them under herself before gently guiding her from the surgical suite.

The girls standing in the waiting room stared at her, looking for some sign of what was in store for them. Orphelia wanted to warn them. She wanted to tell them it was horrible, the worst pain you could possibly imagine. She wanted to tell them to run. When she took a breath deep enough to speak, a thousand needles stabbed her throat, and she could only gasp and fall forward into Mummy's waiting arms. She was carried home, weeping silent tears of pain and betrayal.

This would be Orphelia's first memory.

———

Orphelia used her brother's workshop at night, while the family slept, tinkering and testing, researching and revising. The blueprints spread on the workbench looked like the scrawlings of a madwoman, her brother said, but she had not had the benefit of his formal engineer's training. She had only the limited numbers and letters she had learned in school and the small amount of secret training her father and brother had allowed her. It was forbidden to teach girls complex math, physics, or medicine. Still, Orphelia devoured books from the family library when no one was looking. She did her best to absorb them, looking up words in dictionaries and thesauruses, reading every footnote and carefully inspecting and recreating every diagram until she had the best understanding she could manage.

She knew her project was probably futile, especially if anyone were to catch her. But, like many great inventors, she was motivated by spite: every time a prototype failed or research led to a dead end, she would remember the afternoon of her procedure and would try again.

Tonight, she crouched over the workbench, attempting to affix a length of jellyfish tentacle to the inside of a narrow copper ring, using a glue she'd made herself by boiling hooves she'd bought from a butcher. She wore only her bloomers and a camisole, sensitive to the heat of the workshop—or any heat at all—ever since that Monday afternoon. Her hair was swept into a messy chignon and her feet slid around inside her brother's too-big work boots. She'd stuffed the toes with rags and started wearing them after she'd ruined a pair of silk slippers during one of her experiments, which had earned her a thrashing.

A soft touch on her shoulder made her jump. Her mother stood there, lips pressed together, regretful expression on her face. *Sorry,* she mouthed.

Orphelia's mother was one of the few unfortunate women upon whom the procedure was completely effective. She hadn't been able to say a single word without extreme pain since she was three years old. Of course, breathing was also agony, and she rarely slept as a result, but the medical establishment considered the procedure a total success. Maude was an ideal case written about in textbooks.

I'm busy, Mum. What do you need? Orphelia whispered. She was lucky not to have lingering pain after the wounds of the procedure had healed, and she still had a voice—only a whisper, but better than nothing. From her perspective, anyway. Many people felt differently, especially because she wasn't afraid to use what little voice she still possessed.

Have you thought about Dr. Carver's offer? Maude smiled hopefully. Orphelia's shoulders slumped.

Maude's smile faded. *He expects an answer by tomorrow morning.*

I know.

Maude's hand went to her daughter's arm. *Your father and I were very lucky to marry for love. That's rare. You may not love Dr. Carver, but he can make you comfortable. Papa and I won't be around forever to take care of you.*

Orphelia shrugged and bent over the jellyfish tentacles again. *Quincy and I will look after each other.*

Maude made a scoffing sound that must have hurt and threw up her arms in frustration. She didn't bother to make the rest of the argument. They'd had this talk so many times, Orphelia could play the rest of it in her head. Maude would say that Quincy would want to get married eventually, and what wife would want a man saddled with a spinster sister? Orphelia would reply that Quincy didn't care about getting married and would rather live a quiet life in the countryside with his sister in a house so big they only had to see each other at suppertime. She would add that she was focused on her project, and no husband would let her complete it. A husband would expect her to manage a household and care for children, neither of which held any interest for Orphelia.

And Maude would point out Orphelia's age, which would make her a humiliating failure if she didn't accept an offer soon. Dr. Carver was a good man, and Orphelia would admit that if she were to consider any offer seriously, it would be his, but she simply had no interest in marriage and would not be forced into it.

Maude scowled. For the first time, she mouthed, *This project is ruining your life, O. I should burn it all.* Quick as a snake, she shot across the room and ripped the blueprints off the wall in one swift motion.

Orphelia made a choked sound, the closest thing she could manage to a scream. She ran to Maude and they wrestled over the designs, the paper tearing and crumpling. Orphelia wept and wheezed. Her mother's face was red as she marched from the workshop with her hands full of torn blueprints. Croaking desperately, Orphelia followed her mother into the kitchen and managed one bark of rage as Maude tossed the papers into the smoldering fire in the hearth.

Maude turned to her daughter with fury in her eyes. *You will accept Dr. Carver. I'll send the note in the morning.* She turned and swept upstairs to her own bedroom, and the discussion was ended.

Orphelia knelt in front of the hearth, watching the bits of paper burn. Her mother had never, ever treated her this way before. Of course, Orphelia had never been twenty-seven before. She would already be the oldest bride in the newspaper announcements. And Papa's health had not been good of late. Maude was worried about what would happen to the family if Papa didn't survive his next bout of pancreatitis. Quincy had a brilliant mind for engineering, but was not a great businessman, and would struggle to care for both his sister and mother as the head of family.

Maude wanted the best for her daughter, Orphelia knew. But huge tears still slid down her cheeks as she watched the work of years go up in flames. She clenched her jaw in determination and went upstairs, where she dressed in several layers, packed a few things into a case, and took what money she had squirreled away. She went to the workshop and packed up a few tools, supplies, and the most useful books into the smallest lockbox she could find. She crammed even more into the pockets of her skirts, vest, and jacket.

She didn't know what destination she had in mind as she pulled her black wool cape over her shoulders and swept from the family home. She just knew she couldn't stay here.

———

Orphelia made her way into the heart of town. She had considered calling on cousins or family friends or even school acquaintances to put her up, but had rejected those options, because any of those people would report her whereabouts to her parents. So, she made her way from the posh part of town to the merchant class neighborhoods, where a few people still wandered late at night, mostly stumbling drunks. The flickering streetlamps cast faint, greasy light onto uneven cobbles as Orphelia staggered along in heeled boots. The air smelled like burning oil and raw sewage. The atmosphere made her skin prickle, and every shadow made her gut roil. She carried her mother's warnings about being a woman out in the world alone, and her father's recitation each morning of the murders that had happened overnight while the family slept safely in their beds, dutifully reported in the newspaper. To be out after dark was tempting fate.

Orphelia's heart raced and she almost went home. No one would have to know she'd left. Tomorrow, Maude would send a note to Dr. Carver; he would visit, and a date would be set for her wedding. Soon enough, she would have children of her own. She would have daughters, and when they were three years old, she would march them to the surgery for the procedure.

She pressed on, into the darkness.

As she passed an alley, there was a sound, as of someone being punched and the air gusting from their lungs. Orphelia sucked in a breath and turned to look involuntarily. The darkness writhed with undefined shapes. A second *whuff* convinced her someone was, in fact, being attacked. There! Scuffling and the clicking of heeled boots on the cobbles. She knew she should turn away and flee, but what if a woman was being attacked? A woman who couldn't cry out because the procedure had taken that privilege from her.

Orphelia glanced down the street, hoping for a uniformed officer or a brave-looking gentleman, but saw no one. With a deep inhale for courage, she dropped her case and lockbox into the shadows behind a trash bin. Drawing herself up to her full height, she strode into the alley. She nearly tripped over a piece of wood, which she lifted in her hands as a weapon.

As she approached, the picture became clearer. Several women in black dresses crouched over a prone form. One of them carried a lantern turned down as low as the flame would allow. As they reeled back from the body, one of them cradling something against her stomach, Orphelia saw a man. His eyes were open and staring, his mouth slack-jawed, and his throat torn away, a bloody wreck.

Orphelia had seen corpses before, when her brother snuck her into the anatomy laboratory at his university, but those had been skinned, muscle on display, organs removed, faces covered, flesh cold. This man was still warm. One of his legs kicked and his chest quivered as if he still tried to draw breath.

Orphelia dropped the piece of wood to the cobbles with a clatter. Her gloved hands flew to cover her mouth and she gasped, tears springing to her eyes.

As one, the women turned to her. They were young, younger than she was expecting, with faces ranging from pale to dark, and expressions ranging from panicked to resolute.

Hypatia, one of them hissed to the girl holding the bloody thing. She presented Hypatia with a box and the other girl slipped it inside.

Hypatia turned her attention to Orphelia. With a movement like a scorpion extending its tail, she flicked out a razor, the sort a barber might use to shave a gentleman's beard. Orphelia wanted to run but her legs refused to work. Instead, she whispered *What are you doing? What is this?*

None of your business, Hypatia hissed. *Can you forget what happened here?*

A chorus of rasping voices:
Look at her.

This is the most exciting thing she's ever seen.
She'll never forget.
And she heard your name.
You know what we do to witnesses. Even women.

Orphelia's legs finally worked and she turned to run, but her boots caught in her long cape and the fabric twisted around her ankles. She hit the ground hard, skinning her palms against the rough cobblestones.

The girls were on her like hunting dogs on a fox. Feet kicked her ribs and Orphelia curled into a ball to protect her organs. Fists punched at her arms, shoulder, face and chest. Someone's boot stomped at her face and she rolled away with a screech of terror that came out as a squeak, no louder than the sound made by a mouse.

Hypatia pulled her hair, yanking Orphelia's head back. The razor was cold against the flesh of her throat.

Wait! One girl's whisper was almost normal volume. *Hypatia, wait!*
What?
Look at this! It fell out of her pocket.

Orphelia, trembling with her murderer's blade at her neck, wondered what they could possibly have found. She didn't remember what she had crammed into her pockets. Springs, screwdrivers, books, curls of fine-gauge wire, a vial of jellyfish tentacles. What could possibly interest this gang of murderesses?

The razor fell away and the pressure on her hair increased. Orphelia scrambled up to a sitting position.

Hypatia thrust a book into her face. *Is this yours?*

Orphelia squinted at it. She didn't know. She couldn't see the words on the cover.

Someone turned up the flame in the oil lamp and brought it closer. The book was *Buchanan's Manual of Anatomy*. Orphelia nodded, her eyes finding Hypatia's in the lamplight. The girl's irises were nearly as pale as her face. She looked about fifteen or sixteen years old, with bright flaxen hair. She would have been pretty, if not for a long, ragged scar down one cheek.

What do you know of anatomy? Hypatia asked, breath reeking of stale beer.

Orphelia could only guess why she inquired. The girls looked dirty and bedraggled up close, and they stank of unwashed bodies. Perhaps they were seeking a doctor for their various injuries?

I know it by heart, Orphelia admitted.

Could you do surgery? Hypatia hissed.

Orphelia nodded, grateful the girl asked if she *could* and not if she ever *had.* The answers to those two questions were very different.

———

In a dingy attic room in Madame Pepper's Boardinghouse, the girls arrayed themselves around the room, removing boots and jackets, unlacing corsets, and generally making themselves comfortable. The room was the length of Madame Pepper's entire house. Several mattresses were unrolled on the floor, and various mismatched chests, small tables, and a single dresser missing all its drawers filled the space.

The lamp was turned up to full illumination. The girls cleared the chairs and eating implements from a small table and Hypatia jumped up onto it, seating herself with ankles crossed casually. She presented the lockbox to Orphelia.

Orphelia opened the box gingerly, not sure what to expect. The box was filled to the brim with rapidly melting ice. On top of the ice was a bloody, fleshy lump. Orphelia pulled a pencil from her skirt pocket and prodded it carefully. There was skin, and connective tissue, in the shape of a tube. It was the man's throat, which Hypatia had cut raggedly from his neck, including his larynx.

She suddenly understood what Hypatia was asking. *It can't be done.*

Rage flared in Hypatia's pale eyes and the razor flashed in her hand. *Are you saying you can't, or won't?*

It's impossible.

Why?

The larynx is tangled up with the thyroid gland. It's almost impossible to separate the two.

So?

To remove your larynx and replace it with this one...it would almost certainly kill your thyroid. And you need your thyroid to live.

Hypatia sucked in a breath and her mouth puckered. *How long could I live without one?*

Orphelia recoiled. *No one knows, exactly. It's a mystery what compounds your thyroid releases into your bloodstream.*

The girl raised her chin. *Do it, then.*

Here?

Hypatia nodded.

I can't. This place is filthy. I don't have medical tools, or anesthesia…

We have those things, another girl rasped.

Venus is a nurse, Hypatia whispered. *She can assist you.* Her hand went to her throat, massaging it, as if even this small amount of speech caused her pain.

Orphelia steeled herself, shaking her head. *I can't. It's much too dangerous. You'll die.*

The razor flashed to her throat. The girls surrounded her, their bodies pressing uncomfortably close. *No, she won't,* Venus hissed. *What happens to her, happens to you.*

Orphelia weighed her options. She could confess to her lack of medical experience right now. But if she did, these crazed girls wouldn't hesitate to throw her from the roof of Madame Pepper's Boardinghouse. Performing the surgery was the best choice she had. At least there was a chance Hypatia might survive, and thus Orphelia might as well.

She sighed, the exhalation scraping past her own mangled vocal cords. She raised her chin, removed her cape with a flourish, and accepted the box of excised human flesh.

———

Orphelia tried to perform the surgery quickly. Breathing through a tube could not be comfortable, even with anesthesia, and she feared Hypatia waking while she was still removing the remains of her larynx or inserting the new one. Her hands shook as she stitched the new larynx in place. The organ was too large for the girl's slim neck, and it would probably bulge and cause her pain forever.

At least she could be proud of how she managed to preserve

Hypatia's thyroid, coiled around the front of her neck like a fat snake, protecting her throat. If they could keep her from getting an infection, she might actually survive this reverse procedure.

When she finished stitching Hypatia's throat closed, Orphelia collapsed into a puddle on the floor.

She lives, for now. Venus announced authoritatively in the heavy silence, her voice nearly as loud as a man's softest speech, her fingers pressing into Hypatia's wrist. The other girls turned wide eyes full of wonder to the surgeon weeping on the floor.

There was still so much that could go wrong, but Orphelia didn't point this out. She let the girls undress her, pull a clean nightgown over her head, and guide her onto one of the stinking mattresses. She fell asleep staring at a mouse hole in the wall.

She woke sometime later to someone plying her with warm, salty broth. She gulped it down without opening her eyes more than a crack, and then went back to sleep again. Exhaustion was like a heavy weight around her ankles, pulling her underwater.

When she woke again, it was to the sound of excited chatter. One of the girls crouched beside Orphelia's mattress. *You awake?* The girl mouthed.

Orphelia nodded and pulled herself to a sitting position. Her limbs were heavy as stones and her stomach growled. Her mouth tasted like she'd been eating roadkill. *How long have I been asleep?*

The girl held up three fingers.

Orphelia started and scrambled to her feet, casting about the dark room. *How is Hypatia?* Girls and women dressed in black crowded the attic space.

The girl offered her a black blouse, skirt, and waist cinch much like the ones she wore.

No, thank you. I'd rather wear my clothes.

Sold, the girl mouthed. She tapped her chest and mouthed, *Winifred.*

Sold? Anger and fear lanced through Orphelia's chest. *You sold my things?*

Winifred shook her head. *Not me.*

Venus appeared from the crowd. *Your things were sold to benefit the revolution. These clothes should fit, Doctor Waverly.*

Orphelia started again. She wanted to ask how they knew her surname, but then she thought about her travel case embossed with her initials, the velvet jacket with her first name embroidered on the breast, and the delicate lace waves sewn to the hem of her cape. It wouldn't take too much work to put those pieces together if you were clever.

I'm not a doctor, Orphelia protested.

You are now. Venus offered Orphelia a slim pamphlet printed on ivory paper.

Dr. Orphelia Waverly has performed the greatest miracle: returning human speech to the female throat! The pamphlet proclaimed. *See the wonder in the flesh when Hypatia Crane-Hemsby SPEAKS at sunset on April 26th on the steps of City Hall.* Beneath this, in a flowing, cursive script, was written: *Government Men and Church Elders, we recommend you cease and desist robbing girls and women of their voices, or WE WILL TAKE YOURS.*

There were two women sketched in the middle of the pamphlet, with remarkably good likenesses: Orphelia and Hypatia. Orphelia's stomach dropped and her skin went suddenly clammy.

You've ruined me, she gasped.

Venus clapped a strong hand on Orphelia's arm. *No, friend. We've made you the key to the revolution.*

Orphelia folded herself back onto the mattress, staring at the pamphlet. Winifred quietly placed the clothes beside her. The two women turned to join the others, who were making their way downstairs.

Wait, Orphelia called after them, her loudest call a harsh croak.

Venus turned back.

*April 26th would be in only...*her muddled brain tried to do the math, but she couldn't remember what date it had been when she fled her family home.

Three days, Venus said.

Will Hypatia be able to speak by then? That's so soon. The swelling...

Venus stared down her nose at Orphelia. *She heals quickly. She'll be fine.* And then Venus made her way to the ladder and down, leaving Orphelia alone in the suddenly drafty attic in only a nightgown.

Orphelia dressed quickly. The blouse was tight, and the black skirt and petticoat were much too long and would require hemming. The only item in her possession unsold by the revolutionaries were her boots, which were a dark enough green to appear black, especially under these too-long skirts. Winifred had left her a black ribbon to tie up her hair, as the other girls did, but Orphelia drew the line there. She raked her fingers through her tousled mane and hoped some few of her curls still remained. Without a mirror, it was difficult to tell. She imagined she must look frightful and couldn't help thinking what her mother would say. She could almost see Maude's lips mouthing, *You really must make more of an effort, O.*

Tears rose to her eyes at the thought of her mother. She dashed them away. Her stomach rumbled again and she moved to the ladder, throwing her legs over so she could climb down.

Rough hands caught her and pushed her back up into the attic. *What are you doing?* She demanded when she regained her breath, staring down the ladder at two black-clad women. One was small and wiry, and the other was tall and stocky, like a farmgirl from a provincial tale.

The small one shook her head slowly and pointed to the attic. The communication was clear enough: Orphelia was to remain upstairs.

I'm hungry, Orphelia complained, pressing her hand to her stomach.

The small one nodded at her companion. The larger woman moved in front of the ladder and stared up at the captive while the smaller one slipped out of view, hopefully in search of sustenance.

With a sigh, Orphelia settled her skirts around her like a nest and waited.

———

Hypatia appeared the following afternoon with a group of new recruits. A black scarf was tied around her throat. She sat beside

Orphelia on her mattress and handed her a pasty wrapped in paper, still warm.

You sold my things, Orphelia whispered.

Not the important things. Smirking, Hypatia rose and went to the drawerless dresser, pulling out some clothes and dumping them on the floor so she could reach deep inside and remove Orphelia's lockbox.

Orphelia snatched it from her hands and opened it eagerly, fingers gliding across the implements and prototypes, unpacking each with tender care. Tears of overwhelming relief stung her eyes.

You should let me see your throat, Orphelia whispered, closing the lockbox and hiding it under her skirts as she reseated herself on the mattress. She unwrapped the pasty and tucked in gratefully.

Venus is caring for me. Hypatia's words were barely a whisper, inaudible over the crinkling of the paper pasty wrapper. Fortunately, Orphelia had a lot of experience reading lips.

Is Venus a nurse the way I'm a doctor?

Hypatia shrugged and frowned. She didn't look Orphelia in the eyes as she untied the scarf and let it fall away. Hypatia's face was pale, but her neck was red and splotchy with purple bruising that was visible even in the dim light streaming in the filthy attic window. Her neck was swollen and lumpy, straining Orphelia's neat stitches.

Orphelia shook her head. *You should be in bed. You need to rest.*

I feel fine.

You don't look fine.

I'm recovering very well.

You could die!

Hypatia turned to Orphelia, settling those eerie, near-translucent eyes on her. *We're all going to die. When I'm gone,* she paused to wince and her fingers came to her throat, hovering as if she wished she could touch the tender flesh, but didn't dare. *Take care of them.* She nodded to the many girls in black who had swarmed up the ladder to stuff the attic, more girls than Orphelia had seen up here before.

Orphelia realized, then, that Hypatia intended to martyr herself. And, apparently, she was leaving her recruits in Orphelia's care. *Why me?*

But Hypatia shook her head, unable to say more for the pain.

Orphelia helped her tie the scarf around her neck again. And then Hypatia beckoned the new recruits downstairs and they were gone, leaving Orphelia alone to wonder why she had been chosen as the caretaker of this ragtag motley. She lay down on the mattress again and realized she couldn't even smell the stink of it anymore. She wondered if the stink had become a part of her.

All this, she thought wryly, because she wouldn't marry Henry Carver.

———

Winifred collected her on the third day and threaded her arm through Orphelia's as they walked down the cobbled streets, like bosom friends rather than captor and captive. The fresh air, even reeking as it did of raw sewage and stagnant rainwater, was a balm to soothe Orphelia's restlessness.

Hypatia and her girls now numbered in the hundreds, and when Orphelia and her escort arrived, they had already taken control of the courtyard before the City Hall steps. A crowd had gathered and more were arriving, attracted to the hustle and bustle like flies to a corpse. Hypatia stood on a wooden crate and untied her scarf, holding it in place as the sunset illuminated her black dress and ghostly white skin in gold and pink.

A policeman stood toward the back of the crowd, taller by a head than anyone else there. "You, get down from there," he called.

"Are you ready to see?" Hypatia asked. Her voice was as loud as any man's, but it made Orphelia gasp. It was higher, more musical, like the trill of a flute or a bird. It was beautiful, even if there was a pained rasp behind it.

The crowd thrust their arms into the air. They were mostly women, except for the police officers gathering around the edges of the throng, so their shouts were not so much a ringing chorus as a hiss, like the sound of a giant snake, with a few impassioned squeaks and choked grunts. A few reporters at the back of the crowd scribbled notes and an artist frantically sketched the scene in charcoal.

Hypatia pulled the scarf away with a triumphant flourish. Her throat was red, lumpy, purple and blue in places, green in others, horribly bruised and probably oozing something, but the sutures held. Her voice rang out. "If you take our voices," she pointed at the policemen now pulling batons from their belts, "we will take yours!"

The assembled women hissed their approval and Hypatia's scarf fluttered dramatically to the ground. Hypatia reached into her pocket and pulled out her trusty silver razor, lifting it high, so the sun's last rays limned it gold. Orphelia's breath caught. She was reminded of Durandar, Legbiter, and Excalibur.

Winifred had brought Orphelia close now, close enough that she could see Venus hovering directly behind Hypatia, waiting to catch her should she collapse. Arrayed around the crate on which she wobbled were a dozen girls in black, like dogs ready to attack. Orphelia turned to regard the crowd and watched as hoods and hats were thrown off, and black-clad women and girls turned their backs to Hypatia so they could face the police officers ringing the gathering. A tense silence fell over the courtyard for an instant as the sun slipped below the horizon, plunging them all into the hazy gray of early evening lit only by the dull golden glow of streetlamps.

A shot rang out, and blood erupted from Hypatia's throat, a long crimson scarf, nearly black in the darkness. She tumbled gracefully from the crate.

The riot began.

Winifred joined her sisters, a razor flashing in her hands as she rushed a policeman who fumbled with his pistol. Chaos exploded all around Orphelia. Unarmed, she could only stand watching as the revolutionaries and the police collided, razors versus batons, fists versus pistols. The men shouted curses and commands, but the women were silent, their voices stolen, their demands spoken in a language of blood and bruises.

Orphelia turned back to the crate where Hypatia's body lay sprawled. Venus was trying to drag her down. Orphelia ran to help, and together they pulled their leader's body to the ground. Venus sought a pulse at Hypatia's throat, her wrist. But she shook her head and lowered Hypatia's eyelids.

They shot her, Orphelia rasped.

She chose her fate, Venus answered.

We need to get out of here.

Back to the attic. Do you know the way?

Orphelia nodded and took off running up the City Hall steps, hoping she could perhaps discern a path back to the sidewalk through the riot from above.

Instead, she saw a familiar figure standing in the teeming crowd, perfectly still, her eyes locked on Orphelia. Orphelia blinked. It was her mother, Maude. Orphelia deflated for a moment, confused, fearful, expecting to see disappointment or perhaps even hatred in her mother's eyes.

But the only emotion on Maude's face was hope. She mouthed, *Me next.* Her hand fluttered to her throat.

Two futures spread out before Orphelia. In one, she married a doctor. In the other, she was the doctor.

She extended her hand to her mother and beckoned her to follow.

JACK

Linda Nagle

10

This is only to be expected, but halfway between Beautiful and Terrifying is the end of tomorrow and the beginning of the man. It must be—he feels it. This is the way of the dark and the day, so he feels it. He feels it in every fibre, here in the pathway of last year's kitchen. Here, in this rotten old spot where he'd stood then and stands now, simultaneously clutching and disregarding a cold mug of undrunk coffee while evaluating life and himself and paying little attention to the swash of flies decorating the window: damn those buzzing, undulating curtains.

A moment ago, he'd felt it from the place of water and aesthetic effort, evacuating nothing more than remorseful thoughts. And he'd felt it from yesterday's living room, and last week's garage, and wherever he'd happened to be that crisp, autumn night—the autumn night that had begun the beginning.

But before all that, and before all this, things were nothing if not dull, and Jack McAndrew's ordinary life was arranged according to conformity and acquiescence. And as for people—ugh. People and their ways. Call scripts at the office, measured offerings of politeness at supermarkets, and an obligatory tolerance for his father. But here, now, a second brush of the teeth is required to rid his mouth of the coffee taste that isn't there. This means he must return to the bathroom. And to return to the bathroom he must pass through the bedroom. And to pass through the bedroom he must rid himself of the words and the sheets and the images that play on repeat there in the room and here in his head; it is here, in his head, that he feels it the most. But what of conversation? *That can wait,* he thinks. *The conversation will come.*

This is all in accordance with procedure, so he takes a look at the closed bedroom door. No, not at it—*through* it. Through, behind, and into its bad, bad blackness; a terrible undoing he doesn't see. Not yet. No, not yet, although the late-night choices have been made. Beyond terminology and temperance, all the yesterday soldiers of freedom and fortune are somehow on their way to one or more of the many other sides. Just as there shall forever be an infinite number of possible futures, so shall there be an infinite number of irretrievably impossible people. Impossible people just like Jack.

Spinning into the fibres of medium density, the fabric of wood and life, he thinks himself through the door with stillness and calm, thought-by-thought, molecule-by-molecule. He doesn't see—won't see —the smells; neither can he taste the boudoir colours: raucous reds rapidly on their way to quiet brown, decaying rainbows mere breeding grounds for the busy sounds of green bacteria. This is only to be expected when a person has a petri dish for a bed.

9

Hunger must have taken priority over convention, he supposes. Now, though, on a neglected nightstand next to an experimental bed, an accumulation of stories: encrusted books, a circumference of dried-out, gone-off noodles and a furry green mass that quite possibly originated as overcooked, undereaten chicken. Deep in his gut: bad, bad blackness from a terrible, terrible restaurant. He can still taste it in the yesterday-things clinging to his teeth. And he's out of toothpaste. This is the way of the dark and the day, so he is out of toothpaste.

With words and sheets—where tales once crept into his ears—a nightly reading had, until recently, kept him going. The reading had stopped. The books had stopped. No words, no voices, no existence. Although the conversation is yet to come, he is no longer who he was, quite unlike those books—paper pages don't age in the same way putrefaction happens to ... *happen.* On board his—*their*—shelves, stories for the remorseful. Tales of fitful, littered pasts, badly-plotted and void of depth.

Congealed and mad afflictions their campaign, the books have steadily become their own embers through burning, burned pages and hopeless poultry. Everything's still consumable the next day, though, as long as it's been covered up overnight.

Thinking himself over to the side of the bed, Jack looks through the photographs on the nightstand. No, not through them—*at* them. His husband is frozen into a frame there, a handsome man of thirty, thirty-seven, or forty-two, burned into the thing with a hint of a smile and the faintest taste of regret. Regret, like their apartment, is wet with damp passion and soiled with dishes and life. It would have been easy to load the machine, but other things had taken priority.

8

The strangeness does not discriminate. It happens in the day, at night, and at every point between Asleep and Awake. That hypnagogic soul is somebody else's now, and his dreams are no longer his. His legs move through the pain, through the months, through anything but his own volition. People, machines, perhaps —who knows? Not him, no. No, not him.

Jack ventures outside with a thought, a hobble, and a furry mouth —and without stopping to lock the door behind him. Why bother? This is all in accordance with procedure, so he clambers into an unfastened car whose metallic exterior is a vision of perfection: washed and waxed seventy times a week—or perhaps even seventy times a day. Nobody dares steal around here. There are consequences for everything, so nobody dares. Everything has a sticker. A barcode. Identification. All things are traceable these days. And traces lead to origins. Culprits. Sometimes he'll lock the car out of habit, considering the old town—but now that he's in the new one, he reminds himself to remember that it doesn't matter if he forgets.

He also has a habit of forgetting how he arrives at work. Suddenly, he's *there*. He's just there. Every day, a lapsed passenger on an overlooked journey. And once he is there, at the office, the woman who brings the buns brings the buns. She already knows which one he will have—the same cinnamon roll as always. Lightly drizzled with lemon icing and topped with bitter shavings of waxy rind, it lands on his sad old desk with the feeblest promise of the faintest taste: a moment's sweetness to replace the cemetery bitterness of a desk that is all paperwork and no space. No space. All paperwork and no space.

And no conversation, either—not yet. Now is not the time.

In an unforgiving corner by a disregarded coffee machine, a sodden box of decaying donuts, congealed and mad. Twelve items, one design: frosted in white with eager pink sprinkles, crunch where there shouldn't be crunch, and a graveyard flavour. Two trays of sandwiches, lined up to perfection but for their curled, cardboard crusts, each and every pair of triangles offering the same filling: egg mayonnaise (which is more like mayonnaise egg, truth be told). But he must be selective before the conversation comes. A floppy paper plate recommends a decaying jacket potato that fails to recognise the benefits of aesthetic effort and whose cheese has solidified into cold, greasy globules and separated itself into fat and—fatter. *It'll do*, he thinks. *I'm hungry*. He must be—he feels it. He thinks he feels it.

This is all in accordance with procedure so he considers thinking about eating. He thinks about considering it. Two bites prove a pair too many, repeating on the edge of his nerves, gnawing and irritating like that feeling you get when you walk into a room for … what was it again?

A change of scenery, perhaps. A trip to the supermarket? Sure. A trip to the supermarket to purchase the toothpaste in the dark and the day and escape the strangeness. The strangeness that does not discriminate.

7

Forgetting is difficult when every memory is painful. As painful as his legs. Legs that crunch and crinkle, the envy of fallen leaves. And Jack remembers to recall that nobody knows him here. Perhaps this is why the same nobodies avoid him. Taking great pains to move their shaken, shaking selves around him, the other shoppers do not speak (this is not the time for conversation). Neither do they approach, glare, or mutter. For these things and others—many others—he is relieved. Citizens, rushing. Loud, bustling. Ignoring, shouting. Picking, toiling. He is relieved to no longer be a part of it. A part of all this. All that. A part of all this and all that and—shopping. He must go shopping. This is all in accordance with procedure, so he must go shopping.

Collecting a gathering of requirements in his head, he gathers an armful of nothing from a set of shelves stocked with the same old sameness. Everything has its place, and there is a place for everything. Or is it the other way around? What was it his mother used to say? While he considers her parables and mottos and fables, he thinks himself over to a shelf filled with identical boxes, stacked to a uniform height, all looking towards him and saying the same thing: BUY ME. YOU KNOW YOU WANT TO. And he does want to. Oh, he does. But although they speak in unison, he must be selectively segmented. *What do I need?* Only take what you need, Jack. Only ever take what you need.

The checkout, then. The only question this raises, being a self-service facility and all, that of an unconcerned and driverless persuasion, is whether he should re-scan the item it has failed to recognise. He chooses to beckon a member of staff, for his three, ten, or seventeen attempts to communicate with the wrecked technology have proven futile, repeating on the edge of his nerves.

Over she comes. She of the allegiance, she of the dark and the day, she in the uniform of conformity and acquiescence. Hem: the prescribed number of inches below the knee, leaving no space for skin. No space at all. Hair: unbleached and swept back in keeping with her ponytailed brethren and mechanical comrades. Persuasion: programmed to the apex of a pinnacle of a hilt. "What are we having for dinner tonight?" she asks of herself and no other, pressing buttons and scanning her staff ID or scanning her staff ID and pressing buttons—whichever is the way around here. Foregoing his usual measured offerings of politeness, he does not respond as he has no plans for dinner, no plans for her, and no plans to answer this, the oddest of oddball questions.

This is all in accordance with procedure, so the shop assistant stays stuck at the till, confidently talking to nothing and nobody about no one and bus routes and movies and how much cheaper bread is here than the place across the road. Small-talk must be part of the job—as she continues with it in duty-bound abundance, he makes a hasty retreat into the dark and the day with his confusion intact and without his groceries. None of it was important in any case, he supposes: toothpaste, hopeless poultry, and lemons, washed and waxed. *Or waxed and washed?* She, though, *she* keeps talking. She forever has and forever shall. Babble and chatter. If he isn't listening, someone will be. Poor woman—this is probably the extent of her social life. But his moral tolerance does not last; he soon considers her irreverence and thinks her a flake; little more than a distraction.

Back at the office, Jack creeps to the restroom and considers evaluating life and himself from within a locked cubicle, but making sense of things has never been his forte. *Fortes* have never been his forte. Instead, he sits and stands there, thinking, his legs and brain restless. Where to go, where to go?

Mom's. He'll take a trip to Mom's. It's a one-stone situation: fulfil obligations familial, kill time intolerable. Plus: she might have toothpaste. *She might have toothpaste,* he thinks.

Outside of love and respect and nature and humanity, he has never been particularly fond of his mother. He has to say everything thrice, ten or seventeen times. And she has never been fond of that sweaty apartment of his, where she's sure he sits on his backside all day with bottomless beer and unswitchoffable wi-fi just so he can drink himself silly and feed himself to the bored. And the fridge is too noisy. And as for that stove of his, it takes far too long to light. But today, he chooses to let her infinite wisdom straight in one ear and right out the other. He thinks away her thoughts and dilutes her words, in that—or a different—order.

"Make sure you feed the cats, son."

Nothing.

"Make sure you load the machine when you get back."

Nothing.

A number of nothings follow a barrage of Mom-isms, a typically dull line of questioning that covers every room and every year of his existence. Did he charge his phone? Did he wipe his ass properly? How about the milk? Is he remembering to check the expiration dates? Does he know that bread is cheaper in this place rather than that? She hopes he is washing his hands before meal times and offers her opinions on his wardrobe choices and says he'd be better off sticking to a pea-sized dollop of mint on his toothbrush.

The next nothing that he says in response, or the something he does not, falls upon ignorant ears. This is not the time for conversation but she keeps talking. She always has. She cannot hear the silence of those who do not respond, so she babbles and chatters some more, about jacket potatoes and chicken and—

—He does not wish to cook for his mother. Or eat with her. Or anybody, for that matter. Not even himself. This is not a hungry day. He could—and would—quite happily avoid Every Person Ever until the end of everything or the start of nothing, whichever comes first.

She might be right about some things, though. She is probably right about many. But in this brutal universe, he is content with discontent. And in any case, he's listened to his parents and society for far too long, having been born and raised the goose. The goose who'd been force-fed a gaggle of down-your-throat showtunes and movies whose central message is *Guy Gets the Girl*—he and his husband are nothing if not fruity proof of an uncinematic life. They are both so handsome and full of charm, though, that either of them could pass for Gay Best Friend, had that been on the cards. Still, for a while, he'd listened to his classic upbringing, which is how he has ended up here, he supposes, classically upbrought. He'd tried girls and God, and girls and God had tried him. But that was then, and this is now. And now is the time, if not for conversation, then to forget all that nonsense. Mind you, with painful memories, forgetting is difficult.

6

Here, in this tomorrow, in this banal universe of brutality and underestimation, the gaslit undertones and magnified overtones of existence have backed Jack into the nooks of the deepest recesses, with crannies far darker and unforgiving than corners could ever hope to be. Forgetting today and paying little attention to apathy, he takes a trip forward via the shortest journey back: out of his maternal bindings and down the steps, beyond terminology and temperance. He's read all the books, so the street is library-quiet—he can hear a mouse drop, or a pin squeak, or whatever the saying is.

The people pass and stop and stop and pass, as is the way of the dark and the day. Sometimes, they speak; no times, he hears. A person would have to listen in order for that to happen, and now is not the time for conversation. What he sees, though, is only to be expected for a town of this nature.

And he sees it all. It's all he sees.

How will Jack ever learn anything about himself, about his future, about his now? Await the conversation, Jack. Just wait.

He does learn—quickly—that every car here is the same. Colour: Same. Shape: Same. Number plate: Same. Unconcerned, driverless vehicles of heavy severity whose aptitude for avoidance serves them well in this, the banal 'verse of brutality and underestimation. Here, in this tomorrow.

5

Despite the vulgarity of his failed purchase and his desire to avoid Every Person Ever, Jack thinks himself into a restaurant and places an advance order two or three or four hours ahead. Chargrilled chicken, mixed chow mein, spring rolls and sauce. Oh—and prawn crackers. *That'll do. No time for a banquet—this is not a hungry day.* And while he awaits satiation, for one-hundred-and-twenty, one-hundred-and-eighty, or two-hundred-and-forty minutes, he knows it's time to settle down. He knows. He thinks he knows.

Love, he fears, has overlooked or bypassed him so far, perhaps having seen him coming and taken a detour. But he must be selective. Today is the day his new phone is due to arrive, replacing the old, shattered bones of its predecessor. And when it does, he will regain his access to on-line love.

He thinks himself there, to swiping time. Whichever direction is in the affirmative, he swipes that way and twitches his restless legs as he does so. A familiar, handsome man of thirty, thirty-seven, forty-two, it doesn't matter—Mark is hot. He also enjoys the same things, including but not limited to That Show Everybody Else Hates—and he's never even *seen* a single Star War. This one might be a keeper. Not like that other guy. Or the dog-loving oddball with the ears. *Oh, man. Those ears*—black inside. The hips of a woman. Skinny, hairless creature, the peach-fuzz body of a Sphynx cat—but nowhere near as good-looking.

For all of three seconds, Jack chastises himself for body-shaming—or thinking about it—and sends a message to Mark. There could be a relationship, or even a conversation there, despite the vulgarity.

4

Introspection is not the order of the evening but he wants to employ a little of it anyway—it's something he must do in order to be good enough (a thing he does not think he has ever been—although Mark would be sure to disagree). He is sure he knows how to go about it, too. He has read all the books. All the drivel and the dirge. All part and parcel of the encrusted, burned pages etched into his mind and under his skin. He knows how it works. He thinks he knows how it works in the dark and the day. He knows the rules, the structure, the plot-points, the beats—he thinks.

A mirror. That's what he needs. That's what he thinks he needs. That's how characters are bound—duty bound—to assess themselves and their situations, right? That's how they see things they've never noticed before, yes? Bookwomen notice more than storymen, it has to be said. They notice how water droplets form and fall as they take a shower. They notice their own breasts for the first time ever—*And they wash*, he thinks, *as if they have not washed ten thousand times before, taking in every curve and taking their sweet, wet time to appreciate their fine selves.* But what of men? How will Jack ever learn anything unless he finds himself looking into the reflective surface of the bathroom cabinet and having a conversation with himself—or taking a shower to assess his bodily beauty? No—Jack's smarter than that. *I'm smarter than that*, he thinks. He soon comes to feel that this is not the exposition he deserves. He thinks he knows he realises that this is not the way of the dark and the day. This is not in accordance with procedure. And introspection is not the order of the evening.

3

Here, it is black inside. Here, in a head. Here in a head in a cool room in a dark and hideous building on the unfrequented street, it is black inside. From somewhen: a voice. Two. Three. Four or five, maybe. It's hard to make them out when it is black inside.

2

It is time for the conversation.

1

Mark takes a slow, quick walk with his mother-in-law. Hurrying nowhere gradually, they take their time in a rush, making small-talk to help pass the sixty-second, hundred-mile trip. It's a beautiful, terrifying day—or perhaps somewhere in between the two.

He turns to face Mrs McAndrew. "The food is terrible here, don't you think?"

She agrees. "One type of donut," she says, "and did you see the state of those egg sandwiches? I wouldn't feed them to the dog!"

"Ugh, yes. And my coffee was cold." It will stay that way, too. Cold, undrunk, disregarded.

"Ah, poor you. You're a good lad, Mark. And a great dad, too. I'm so glad our Jack met you before—"

"—I'm glad I met him, too."

A few more steps and they'll reach the ward, a place they shall visit for the first, seventieth, or last time, where they will continue their conversation, not knowing what else to do, precisely as they have done every week for the last however-long. And once they arrive, as ever, they shall discuss, as expected, all manner of everything—from feeding the cats to loading the machine. Shopping, too. "Did you know that bread is much cheaper at that place on the corner?" Turns out, he does. He's heard it all before. Many times.

Mark swats at a fly near the window, and misses. It lands on the curtain between this bed and the next, but wings itself away as a woman in blue makes her way over to the bed to manipulate Jack's limbs. He's been here for a month, a year, whatever—it makes no difference to immobile minds.

"Thank you, love," says Mark. "I'm very grateful."

"Oh, it's all part and parcel. It's my job to look after him. We wouldn't want those nasty bedsores coming back, now, would we?"

Oh, those greens, those yellows, and the reds—they'd already been on their way to brown before anybody had noticed. And the smell! A smell so bad you could see it.

"If you would just excuse me for a second, I'll be right back to replace the drip. We can't have him getting dehydrated again, can we?"

"Have you charged his phone?" asks Mum. "Just in case he wakes up. And have you wiped his—" She cannot ask the question. *It is too personal*, she thinks.

The blue woman makes her exit, and Mark makes a suggestion. "Shall we read to him some more?"

"I don't know, love. All those books are a bit rubbish, you know. No plot to speak of."

"I'm pretty sure we've read them all already, too!"

As Mark contemplates the collection of paperbacks, his heart gathering old dust and new stories, he has an obvious thing to state, so he states it. "I don't even know if he can hear us anymore."

But the man in white knows. The man in white—the third or fourth or fifth person in the room—thinks he knows. There's no brain activity, now. What little function there once was has now faded to nothing. There is proof of this, and there are reasons scientific, but none of those things matter when a person has a petri dish for a bed.

They comb his hair and brush his teeth, for he cannot. They remove the experimental build-up of fur and plaque from all his yesterdays—from all his yesterweeks. Unable to spit, they must assist with that, too. As they do, they speak in stilted sorrow—a conversation nobody wants to have. It's all part and parcel, though, of helping him. Helping him to breathe and to exist, and to comb his hair and keep his mouth fresh when he cannot.

The metal frame of his bed a vision of perfection, it is washed down seventy times a week, or even seventy times a day. Cannulas and catheters and wipes and sheets, tools to stall the inevitable. Bandages and dressings, a priest for a blessing. A few sad weeks ago, Jack's mother even tried a medium for size. Why, only she knew. Well, she and Jack. They both knew.

But there was and there is no divination to be had, and certainly no divinity. A godless place now, this ward. And rightly so; everything is about the science. No time for nonsense. No time. No space, either. It's all paperwork and no space.

"It is time to have the conversation, Mrs McAndrew."

"I'm sorry, what?"

"We need to discuss our—*your*—plans."

"Say again?"

"In accordance with procedure, we must discuss—"

"I'm sorry—before you go on, do you mind if we open the curtains? It's not right for it to be dark in the day."

"I do apologise, Mrs McAndrew. Regrettably, it seems there is little more we can do for your son. But there are ways—"

"—No," she says. "You must ask Mr ... *Mark*. Ask Mark. He's my son's husband. His next of kin."

Oh, what a selection of choices are laid out in front of him. A choice selection of life and death and everything in between. There's no hope, say the team. There's every hope, says Jack's mother.

As they think of Jack and themselves, Jack thinks of donuts and checkouts and car after car and cold coffee and flies and books and bedrooms. Bedrooms where, amidst the hunger and the bad, bad blackness, amongst the terrible restaurants and failing machinery and the conversations with his mother, sleep has been forgotten. Sleep is horrific. Sleep is where you go to forget—

—But no matter, no matter. In amongst the cold coffee and the decaying donuts, all the late night choices have been made, not by Jack but for him. What is best for him now, though, lies beyond mother and husband, far beyond terminology and temperance. All the soldiers of freedom and fortune in their noble, just causes, are on their way to one of the many other sides. It happens to us all, somehow. But, just as there is an infinite number of possible futures, so there will always be an infinite number of irretrievably impossible people, impossible to retrieve.

Jack is one of those people. Simultaneously alive and dead until his state is revealed by the shoddiest and most expensive technology that paints only half the picture. *No activity,* they think. "No activity," he thinks he hears, as he considers toothpaste and coffee and how the two do not go together. He considers static black caverns and bathrooms and combs and doors that open onto every nothing. He thinks about thinking some more, but rests a little, now. He thinks he is thinking about resting. His temperature thirty, thirty-seven, forty-two.

They say they will keep going for a while longer with drugs and machines and experimental surgery and physiotherapy while they await the inevitable. *It's for the best,* they think. "It's for the best," they say. But no matter, no matter—"Jack can't feel a thing," and it will be over soon in any case.

After all, there is no activity here, halfway between Beautiful and Terrifying.

They know what's best.

They think they know.

They think.

AVOCATION

Lucy A. Snyder

The worst thing I ever did? Oh, my. That's quite the question for a first date!

But I get it: we're both too old for trivia like our favorite movies or cocktails. You want to see me prick myself on the needle of my moral compass. See what colors I bleed.

Oh, honey, no ... I wasn't calling *you* old. You're, what, fifty? Prime of your life! Want some wine?

There you go. As for me ... I guess it's not ladylike, but I don't mind thinking of myself as older. Not like I'm a hag or something, but ... I've been around. Wisdom. Experience. Skills. Ought to count more than how perky my tits are, right?

Right?

C'mon, don't make that face.

Oh, it's the merlot? Too bitter? Okay, how about a martini? One sec.

So, your question. Stop me if you've heard about this: Allfine Insurance, 2015.

Not ringing a bell? Really? It made the national news for at least five seconds, and they *are* a competitor of your firm ....

Right. You're very busy. Who has time to watch the news?

So, let me give you my personal prospectus. I got my BS in nursing right after high school because I wanted to help people. I maintained a 4.0 grade point average, got a great job right after graduation with Cary Hospital in Columbus, Ohio. Things were good for two years.

But then, I was helping a 40-year-old stroke patient — huge guy: former Bengals linebacker with CTE — and he stumbled and I instinctively tried to catch him. Fell right on me. Fractured my L1, L2, and a couple of ribs when we hit the floor. My back was wrecked, and hands-on nursing was clearly not something I could do anymore.

My medical bills and college loans weren't going to pay themselves, so—after I could walk again, I had to find another job. I tried telemedicine for a while, but I found it super frustrating. Then a colleague told me Allfine was hiring nurses as medical claim reviewers. I thought, "Why not?" and applied.

They hired me and five other nurses, and at first it seemed ideal. The pay was amazing, and the company had great perks like Aeron chairs and a fully-equipped onsite gym. I was determined to get my mobility and function back. Being able to do my PT throughout the day was huge.

Another great thing was that I met Willow. She was one of the nurses in my training cohort. One of the smartest, kindest, most decent people I have ever known, period. And she was so much fun! Everyone loved her. I fell for her really hard, and before I knew it we had an apartment in Victorian Village together —

Yes, I'm bi.

... No, I don't do threesomes. May I finish my story? Thanks.

Willow was a shining light at that company. The others in my cohort? Not so much. The worst was a guy named Rodney. He'd been a corpsman in the Marines, and rumor was he witnessed a massacre in Iraq. Now, clearly this man had PTSD, and a lot of insecurities that he was trying to compensate for, so I tried to be patient with him.

But he was just such an *asshole*. Loud, abrasive, bragged all the time about how he was screwing people out of their benefits because he'd found some small technical problem in their claims. He took joy in keeping people from getting health care! Every day I wanted to shake him and ask, "What is *wrong* with you?"

Our 6-month reviews came up. Willow and I ... got mediocre scores. Rodney, of course, couldn't keep his mouth shut about how well he'd done. So, I went to my supervisor on the QT and was like, "What gives?"

Then I find out that, contrary to *everything* in our training documentation, contrary to *everything* the company tells their customers ... they really wanted us to reject as many claims as we could. Didn't matter if it was a newborn baby with a malformed heart valve. Didn't matter if it was a mother of five with cancer. Find a defect in the claim? Reject it, and don't offer advice on fixing it.

Be silent in the face of other people's pain and misery.

Willow and I were appalled. This was the *worst* bait-and-switch. We honestly felt like our life mission as human beings was to help people. Except that wasn't the job. We talked about walking away, but we both had mountains of debt.

And she told me, "The money shouldn't matter this much, but it does. If we quit, they'll just hire someone else to do what they say. And we won't be able talk about what Allfine is doing because of the NDAs we signed. But if we make our supervisors happy, we can get promotions and work to change the company from the inside."

So naïve, right? But she seemed so certain, and I wanted to believe it was possible.

We both stuck with it for ten years, trying to do what the company wanted while trying to help as much as we could ... and it was really, really difficult. We'd turn down claims that we desperately wanted to approve, and it killed us a little each day.

In my heart, I'm convinced that's why Willow developed an aggressive triple-negative breast cancer. I think working there poisoned her on a cellular level.

She worked as long as she could, then went on short-term disability. I knew what was happening, what was *going* to happen, and couldn't stop any of it. I shaved her head for her so she wouldn't have to watch it all fall out. Held her hand during chemo treatments. Rubbed her back when she was puking her guts out afterward. I watched the woman I loved more than my own life waste away and there was nothing I could do.

I got fired about a week before she died. It was because of all the leave I'd taken. Not officially, of course ... I'd filled out all the FMLA forms, and nobody would find a damn technicality in *my* paperwork.

But Ohio has at-will employment, so they don't need a reason to lay you off.

And it wasn't just me: they dumped about a dozen other employees. Their brass boy Rodney was one of them, probably because he said the quiet parts out loud too much. I hate to admit it, but knowing he was out of a job, too ... it was a little slice of schadenfreude pie. I was so sick with grief and anger, any other emotion seemed refreshing no matter how sour.

After Willow was gone, I lost our apartment and had to sell off most of our belongings. Ended up in a crappy one-bedroom in North Columbus. Anger just built and built inside me. I needed a release valve ... and I didn't have one. I couldn't afford therapy and couldn't go punch bags because of my back.

So, I bought a handgun — a Glock 19 — and took up target shooting. I imagined Allfine Insurance executives' faces on every sheet of target paper I blew to bits at the range.

And that might have been enough ... but the next year was Allfine's 50th anniversary. Suddenly I was seeing their ads on every station, and I couldn't open a local magazine or newspaper without finding a puff piece about all the charity work Allfine executives were doing for the Columbus community: school events, walk/run fundraisers, concerts. All a bunch of heartwarming horseshit, and at the end of every article, all I could see was Willow dying in her hospice bed.

And I thought, "How is it fair that these lying, cheating motherfuckers are still alive and she's gone?"

And then I figured, "Well, I can't bring her back ... but I sure can fix that other part."

I flexed my social engineering skills and got an appointment to see Karen, the HR director, after I spun her administrative assistant Julie a bullshit story about how I was enrolling in an actuary science program and wanted an informational interview about industry needs. Apparently, Karen had been working at the New York branch a whole bunch and had exactly one day available for interviews for like six months. Otherwise, she was booked solid. Karen's office was on the same floor as the main executives' offices. Once I was up in her area, I could just walk down the hall, shooting targets at my leisure, assuming nobody stopped me.

And honestly? I was okay knowing that I'd probably get killed by the police. I missed Willow so much, just hurt so much every day ... I didn't want to live. I felt bad about what it would do to my parents, but they still had my sisters and their kids, you know? They'd get over losing their unemployed queer daughter who most certainly hadn't lived up to her potential.

That said: I was incredibly nervous the day of my "interview." Hadn't slept for like two days and had barely been able to eat. But I stayed cool. I still knew most of the people on the first floor, and so when I arrived, one lady let me in the side door, where they didn't have a metal detector. She took me to a security guard who I also knew; he gave me his condolences about Willow as he escorted me up to the top floor.

Julie met me at the elevators. I remember she was wearing this amazing blue silk dress — I never knew how she always looked so great on what couldn't have been a huge salary. I always admired how put-together she was, but also how kind she was. We were both on the company softball team, and so I'd found out she rescued feral cats and fostered kittens. She seemed like a really good-hearted person. If I hadn't been with Willow, I think Julie and I would have gotten to know each other a whole lot better.

And if Allfine's whole C-suite had been like Julie ... well, I wouldn't have been there that day.

Anyway, she took me down the hall and around the corner the waiting area, which was all done up in Grifter Grey and Beyond Boring Beige. Stare at the walls long enough, and you could feel your will to live draining away.

"Have a seat and Karen will be out to get you herself when she's ready," Julie said, and went back around the corner to her desk.

She left me alone on the uncomfortable reception sofa, my pistol-laden purse heavy against my hip, staring down at a glass bowl full of individually-wrapped wintergreen mints. I love those damn things; I always used to grab one when I was walking by.

And seeing that bowl of mints ... I don't know why that was the thing, but it suddenly grounded me in the moment, and I felt the weight and sheer insane enormity of what I was about to do settle in my guts. I'd lied to Julie—a sweet girl who had never been anything but decent to me—and I was about to kill her boss. She'd hear the gunfire and probably see everyone with their brains blown out.

I was about to inflict an unspeakable amount of survivor trauma on her ... and she didn't even remotely deserve that nightmare.

What the hell am I doing? I thought. *This isn't me. This isn't who I am, and it's not who Willow wanted me to be.*

And so, I stood up, slung my purse across my body and was about to get the hell out of there when I heard the elevator ding open ... and then the stuck door alarm went off.

A moment later, I heard Julie gasp, "What are you doing?"

Then a pop. A gunshot. Holy shit.

The thump of someone collapsing to their knees, then moaning. Julie's voice. She was hurt.

My nurse instincts kicked in, and I hurried around the corner ... and saw that she'd collapsed on her side on the floor. Facing me, her eyes shut in pain. She clutched a bloody wound in her belly. A man in a black suit with a pistol stood above her.

I finally recognized him as he took aim at her head.

Rodney. Fuckin' *Rodney.*

"No!" I shouted at him.

He fired. The 9mm hollow-point round pierced her skull near her left coronal suture and blew out the right side of her jaw. It had to have killed her instantly, but her body jerked and spasmed, and I took a couple of steps toward her, somehow thinking that maybe I could save her.

Rodney pointed the black Beretta M9 at me. I stopped and raised my hands. Everything seemed to slow way down. He moved toward me, and I finally got a good look inside the elevator behind him. He'd murdered the nice security guard, too.

"Jesus Christ, Rodney, how could you kill Julie?" I stammered.

We locked eyes. He had the proverbial thousand-yard stare. Part of Rodney was just *gone.* I don't know if it was his PTSD or if he was on drugs or both. He raised his pistol higher, moving his aim from my core to my face.

"What the hell are *you* doing here?" he demanded.

I was frankly amazed he hadn't shot me yet.

"Interview," I croaked. "Karen only had the one day for interviews."

His gun hand didn't waver. "Julie was part of it. She was *culpable*. We saved them millions, and they threw us away? They need to pay. You see that, don't you?"

I nodded. "I see it."

"You were always nice to me." He lowered his weapon and strode past me. "But don't get in my way again or I will fucking *end* you."

I cannot tell you how profoundly relieved I was. The irony of the whole thing wouldn't hit me until hours later, after I lied to the police, after I lied to the press. But my sudden, inexplicable survival in the face of that bastard wasting the second sweetest woman who ever worked at Allfine left me feeling utterly calm and focused.

When Rodney was past me, his back fully turned to me, I drew my weapon from my purse and shot him in the back of the head.

Let me tell you, it was *much* more satisfying than a paper target. Horrible, yes, but exhilarating. Having that kind of power in your hands ... it's a little addictive, if I'm being honest.

I had gone there that day expecting to die as one of the few female mass murderers in history ... but I lived as a hero. I was nationally famous for about five minutes, as I said. The Second Amendment folks immediately latched onto me as "a good gal with a gun." Once I realized *that* was happening, I made sure to point out that Rodney had murdered two very good people before I stopped him, and everyone would have lived that day if nobody had a gun.

Well. Everyone but Willow, of course. And all the people Allfine had denied critical care to.

So, when I was lying in my bed that night, far too keyed up to sleep, I wondered if maybe I shouldn't have just let Rodney do what he'd gone there to do. They *did* deserve to die, even if he was completely wrong about the reasons.

I'm not the most religious person in the world, but I do believe in fate. I believe there are guiding forces in the universe. I believe individuals are born to do certain things, and a big part of life is figuring out what those are.

Mass murders ... they're no good. That seems obvious, right? But they're blatant acts of terrorism. If your actual goal should be stopping powerful people from doing harm ... well, it's like trying to do cancer surgery with a chainsaw.

That night, I realized I needed a scalpel. Maybe I needed to *be* the scalpel. Either way, I needed to be much, much smarter and deliberate about what I was doing with the unexpected gift of the rest of my life.

And that's where you come in, my dear.

I mean, you didn't think that I would flagrantly violate my Allfine non-disclosure agreement with just *anyone*, right? Surely not. I know you're a man of *supreme* discretion, and your lips are sealed.

That's a little joke. You literally can't talk right now because of the raphides I put in your martini.

I know it seems like our rendezvous at this oh-so-chic hotel suite was a random mutual swipe-right situation ... but I've been planning to meet you for *months*. The policies you've implemented at your insurance company have killed over 1,000 people just this year alone. What a guy! I *had* to put you on my list.

Oh. I've hit a nerve. I can see by the look in your eye that you want to protest that you're not a murderer! You want to tell me it's just business ... but I've done my research. I'd be more than happy to show it to you, but your vision is quite blurry by now, thanks to the modified digitoxin I put in the merlot.

If you don't mind, I'm going to tidy up a bit. Don't want to leave any evidence behind, just in case. But I doubt the police will think this is anything but what it appears to be: a wealthy executive with cardiovascular disease and the high-risk factor of cheating on his wife with Internet strangers had a heart attack in a hotel room. A perfectly mundane, statistically predictable cause of death. Your body will go to the county coroner for a post-mortem examination, of course ... but they're a little overwhelmed by the pandemic right now. They just won't have the resources to look for something they don't suspect is there.

You're my third removal this year. I'd do more if I had some sponsorship, but that's a little tricky. For now, this has to be an avocation.

Don't worry. I won't make you die alone. Company is more than you deserve, but I need to make sure I finished the job.

And between you and me? I *really* enjoy watching the lights go out.

NIL BY MOUTH

Lee Murray

Huian

Huian stepped onto the porch and closed the door behind her. She rummaged in her purse for the key, fingers shaking. The hospital wasn't far. Just a couple of blocks. A fifteen-minute walk at most.

Just fifteen minutes to get help for Mei.

Huian's fingers closed on the key. She pulled it from her purse and fumbled for the lock, banging her hand against the door jamb. Leaning closer, she squinted through the gloom. *Should have left the porch light on.* Too late now. No time. She needed to get help. She'd left it too long already.

But first, she had to get the door locked. She squeezed her eyes shut, then opened them. Key. Lock. Trembling hand.

Concentrate.

At last, the key clinked in the lock. She pushed it home. *There.* Locked. And her granddaughter inside. Her heart clenched. She'd never left Mei alone before, and certainly not when she was sick, but who else was here to go for help? Not her daughter, Lihua, who was working hard to pay for Mei's future and was more than fourteen hours away by plane. Huian hadn't called her. Why make her worry? Huian had thought about phoning the school, but it was nearly ten o'clock. Mei's teacher, the nice lady with streaky dyed hair and the wide smile, would be home with her own family. Even if Huian had the phone number, her English was too limited to make the teacher understand. Not for the first time, Huian chastised herself for not trying harder to learn the language of their host country, for relying on

Mei to read the school news bulletins and fill out the absence questionnaires. Now Mei was paying the price for Huian's laziness. Inside the house, in the stuffy single bedroom, she lay limp in her bed, Hello Kitty covers pulled up to her chin, trembling, tendrils of dark hair plastered to her forehead.

Huian slipped the key into her handbag. Her granddaughter's humours were too hot. Too much yellow bile. Huian had to hurry.

Beyond the porch, it was cooler: raining, the road shiny under the streetlights. Swallowing a cough, Huian started down the stairs: four of them, the number synonymous with death. She usually skipped the last stair, but the rain had made the surface slippery. Huian's foot whipped out beneath her. She yelped. Flailed. She threw out a veiny hand, grasping for the railing, almost wrenching her shoulder from the socket as she grasped the wooden barrier. A splinter stung her palm. Huian clung to the rail, breathing hard, heart fluttering.

She shuffled her feet forward, using the rail to haul herself upright, while her handbag banged back and forth against her chest. She stood a moment, steadying herself.

Must not think unlucky thoughts.

She pushed her handbag into the crook of her elbow, and carefully descended the stairs.

Fifteen minutes to walk to the hospital. Huian hurried into the street.

———

Michael

Michael slowed, pulling up at the lights, savouring the aroma of grease and newsprint in the van's interior. God, he was starving. Late home from a job—a leak in an old villa in one of the city's swankier neighbourhoods—it was a good thing his favourite chip shop had still been open. The teenager on the counter hadn't been too chuffed though, his resentment at having to serve a last-minute customer written all over his face. Well, it was Friday night; the kid probably had other plans. But the store's owner had the last say, and now the pile of hot chips was sweating in their packaging on the seat beside him. Fifteen minutes until he got home, and the smell was doing him in. The lights were taking their own sweet time, so Michael leaned over and wormed his fingers into the paper. He dug around for a chip.

Ouch!

Whipping his burned fingers back, he blew on them.

The lights changed. *Bugger.*

Shaking his fingers, he put the van into gear, just as a car zipped past him in the outside lane, a pixelated blur in the windscreen. But there was someone on the pedestrian crossing.

Michael gulped. The car swerved, hitting the pedestrian, who whirled and tumbled.

Fuck! His heart scudding, Michael bashed on the brakes, his foot planted flat to the floor.

The car zoomed away in a streak of red. A hit-and-run? Or had the driver just not seen the pedestrian in the rain?

The pedestrian! Michael threw the van into park, clicked on the hazard lights, checked the side mirror, then leapt out. He rushed to the front and cursed under his breath. No, no, no. An elderly Asian woman lay just a hair's breadth from the van's tyres.

Oh God. Please don't be dead.

"Hello? Can you hear me? Are you okay?"

The woman worked her mouth like a beached fish, soundless and panicked.

Relief surged through him. She was moving. You don't move if you're dead, right? He strained to remember what the tutor had said at the company's annual first aid sessions. There didn't seem to be any blood. Still, he shouldn't move her. She might have internal injuries. Except, he had to get her out from under there. The van's hazard lights were on, but that didn't mean the van wouldn't get rear-ended by some idiot not paying attention. Plus, the shock was setting in; the woman was already pale and sweaty. The tutor had said shock was dangerous, sometimes as dangerous as the injury.

As gently as he could, Michael gripped the shoulders of the woman's rain jacket and dragged her to the side of the road. While he was moving her, she started talking, incomprehensible garble—

Chinese or Japanese or something—but talking was a good sign, too. You didn't talk if you were dead.

What next?

Call an ambulance. But the hospital was just two streets away. It'd be quicker to take her there himself.

Michael ran to the back of the van and flung open the doors, pushing the pile of plastic pipes out of the way, before returning for the woman.

Still gibbering, she hadn't moved. Not much bigger than a child, he had no trouble lifting her. She didn't argue—at least, not that he could tell—as he lowered her into the back of the van. Michael pulled a bungee cord across her body, fixing the hooks to the shelves that ran on either side of the chassis in a makeshift safety belt. It was just a few hundred metres to the hospital. It would have to do.

Closing the doors, Michael ran to the driver's door and swung into his seat to the waft of his chips. He checked the mirror, pulled into the street.

Another set of lights.

Michael tapped his hands on the steering wheel.

Don't die, don't die.

Next street.

Don't jolt her.

Just past this intersection…

In the ambulance bay, an orderly gestured to him. Michael rolled down the window.

"You can't park here, mate," the orderly said. "This entrance is only for ambulances."

"I've got an injured woman in the back of the van. Car accident."

"Ah, cripes. Can she walk?"

Michael shook his head. "I lifted her into the back."

"I'll grab someone."

While the orderly scurried away, Michael climbed out and opened the rear doors.

Staring at the roof, the woman was murmuring something. *Thank goodness.* She was still alive. "Help's coming," Michael said cheerfully.

"We're at the hospital." Then, feeling awkward, he put his hands in his pockets.

The orderly returned with a gurney and a nurse.

The nurse leaned over the woman. "Hello. I'm Andrea. Can you hear me? What's your name?" He placed his hand at the woman's throat, checking for a pulse. When she didn't respond, he checked her pupils. Then he glanced back at Michael. "What's her name?"

Michael shrugged. "No idea. I just happened to be first on the scene. A driver clipped her on a pedestrian crossing, and she took a tumble."

"A hit-and-run? That's low," the orderly said. He slid a board into the van, lying it flat alongside the injured woman, then clambering in after it. The bed of the van dipped under his weight. "Did you get the licence plate?"

"Nah. It was raining and—"

"—When did the accident happen?" the nurse interrupted. "Has she spoken at all?"

"She was talking when I pulled her off the road. And she spoke just now. Before you arrived. Nothing I could understand, though. I thought it might've been Japanese."

Crouched among the pipes, the orderly was busy fitting a neck brace, but Michael saw his eyes narrow. "You said you saw it happen?" he asked.

"Yeah."

"Where was this, exactly?"

Michael waved a hand, gesturing south. "A couple of blocks away. It was five, maybe ten minutes ago."

What the hell? Did he think Michael had hit the woman himself?

"We need to get her inside." The nurse lowered his head to the woman's ear. "Can you hear me? We're going to move you onto the stretcher now. That way, we can get you into the hospital, so the doctor can take a look at you, okay?" Straightening up, he nodded at Michael. "Can you help slide her over from that side? Just do what I do. Hemi, hold her head stable, will you?"

Following the nurse's lead, Michael grasped the seams of the woman's clothing at her shoulder and hip.

"On three: one…two…three."

They slid the woman's tiny frame onto the gurney. The movement was graceful; still she moaned softly.

The orderly—Hemi—jumped out of the van. He stamped on the wheel-lock to release the gurney. "You should come in," he told Michael, as he wheeled the injured woman towards the bright lights of the emergency department. "Leave your details at the desk."

Yeah, right. So you can report me to the police.

"Sure." Michael closed the rear doors. "I'll park the van, and I'll come straight in."

———

Huian

Huian blinked. The sun was blinding. Painful. Her skin was burning, and she was damp with sweat. At the back of her head, pain surged in and out, in and out. Instinctually, Huian reached a hand across her body and pinched the webbing between her thumb and forefinger, breathing out as the pain eased a little. She needed to get out of this hot sun…

No, wait. It wasn't the sun. Those were lights. She forced herself to focus. She remembered now. It was late and she'd been walking to the hospital to get help for Mei. There was the rain, then the car, and all at once she'd been flung through the air.

Then…*nothing.*

Where was she now? How long had it been since she'd left the house? How long had Mei been alone? Had the little girl woken? Was she calling out for Huian, her fevered body curled into a sparrow's claw? What would she think when Huian didn't come?

She's only ten.

Slowly, Huian turned her head. Her body sagged in relief. The nightstand. The curtain. She was at the hospital. Yes, the hospital. There was the comforting ping of the machines and the low chatter of the staff. Someone must have brought her here. She doesn't recall. It doesn't matter. At least now she could get help for Mei.

One of her hands was numb. Using the other hand, Huian patted the bed for her handbag. It contained the photos of her and Mei, and the paper with all the important information written in English—their names and their address. She would show the doctors the photo, and her address, and they would understand that Mei was at home and needed help.

Except there was nothing for her fingers to touch. Her bag wasn't on the bed.

Ignoring the panic rising beneath her ribs, Huian lifted her head, and examined the shelf in the bedside unit. Her vision blurred. White light blazed behind her eyes. Her throat swelled with bile. Swallowing it down, she dropped her head back on the pillow, pain exploding inside her skull. Her bag wasn't on the shelf. She forced herself to check the chair.

Huian's heart plummeted.

Her bag wasn't here.

Andrea

Outside the cubicle, Andrea handed the paper file to the doctor.

Cath Barker-Hill rolled her shoulders and pulled her pen from the pocket of her scrubs. Andrea noted the grey smudges under her eyes and the tendril of hair escaping from under the protective bonnet. It was fifteen minutes after ten; the doctor's shift was already over.

"So, what have we got?" she asked.

"A woman, around seventy, we think," Andreas replied. "Hit-and-run. A passer-by picked her up and brought her in."

Frowning, the doctor flipped the page up and down. "There's no name."

Andrea shook her head. "No ID either. We don't think she understands English."

"Anyone call for a translator?"

"We would if we knew what language to ask for."

Sighing, the doctor swished the curtain aside and gave the woman a wide smile. "Hello," she said. "I'm Dr Barker-Hill. How are you feeling?" She placed the file on the nightstand and approached the bed.

"Doctor," the woman said.

"Yes," Barker-Hill confirmed. "I'm the doctor."

The woman grasped her wrist. "Doctor," she said again.

Cath Barker-Hill leaned close to the bed. "Yes, I'm the doctor," she repeated. "What's your name?"

The woman responded. Something unpronounceable.

"That's your name?"

The woman replied again; whatever she was saying, it was all Greek to Andrea.

The doctor's voice was gentle. "Is there anyone we can contact for you? Your children, perhaps? A son or a daughter?"

"No son-daughter," the woman said in English, her thin lips pinched.

She clung to the doctor's hand. Andrea's heart contracted. The poor woman. No kids and probably no idea what happened to her. She must be bloody terrified.

The doctor turned to him. "Let's see if Dr Saetang is still out at the front desk. I think our patient might be Thai. I'd really like to order a head scan for that bump—I don't like the look of those pupils—and run a COVID test. But since she's speaking, we really should get her consent first."

Andrea nodded, hurrying away from the cubicle with a swish of the curtain.

———

Huian

Huian woke, groggy and slow with pain. She'd drifted off. Terror flashed through her like the flick of the dragon's tongue.

Mei.

Stupid woman! Huian had gone to sleep when her granddaughter needed her. She scanned the pink-cream walls above the curtains for a clock, but there was nothing—just a brown water stain on the ceiling tiles.

The nice lady doctor was gone. Huian was alone in the cubicle. What was happening? Perhaps they were looking up her name. She'd made sure to say it slowly and clearly so the doctor would understand. She'd said it three times. The other doctor had nodded and left the cubicle. They would look Huian up on the immigration records and when they did, someone would come, and she would tell them about Mei.

But how long would that take? It was late on a Friday night. What if there was no one in the immigration department? What if they had to wait until Monday to find Huian's address? Huian shivered. Monday was too far away. Mei couldn't wait until Monday. When Huian had left the house, the baby could hardly breathe, her little girl's chest working so hard she could no longer talk.

Huian had to hurry. She had to do something.

———

Andrea

"Dr Saetang still about?" Andrea asked at the reception desk.

"Left fifteen minutes ago," Kate said. She didn't bother to look up.

"Bugger. I was hoping to catch him. We still don't have an identity on the patient in 4C and the hospital's interpreter services are closed."

"Did you try these guys?" She pointed her pen at the laminated sign sellotaped to the sliver of wall beneath the counter. It gave the number of a 24-hour translation provider. One hundred and eighty languages. *That should do it.* Andrea moved to the phone.

"Not here! Use the nurse's station."

Andrea scribbled down the number on a Post-It note. He got the service on the line.

"What language do you need?" asked the woman.

"Not sure. She looks Asian."

"Maybe Hindu? That's our fourth most spoken language after English, *te reo*, and Samoan."

Inside his mask, Andrea sucked air in over his teeth. "I don't know. She doesn't look Indian. The doctor thought she might be Thai."

"It's more likely she speaks Mandarin Chinese."

"Okay, let's try that."

"If you can hook your patient up with an iPad or phone when the doctor's there, we can do the translation virtually. But it's Friday night, so might take us a while to find someone with availability."

"Yup. Understood." Andrea gave the woman the number, then hung up. Then he checked the wait room for the van driver in case he had any more information.

A flotsam of anxious parents was juggling stressed out kids, the groups all spaced two metres apart. No sign of the driver, so he bailed up Hemi in the corridor. "Did you see what happened to the van driver? The one who brought in the Asian woman?"

"He said he was parking the van."

"He's not in the wait room."

"Shit," Hemi muttered under his breath. He folded his arms over his chest. "I knew he was shady."

"We still can't communicate with the patient. I wondered if maybe she had a handbag and it was still at the crash site."

"Or maybe he stole it."

"Or maybe he was just too busy trying to get her here that he didn't think to look for it. We should probably have his contact details, anyway—in case of COVID."

Hemi nodded. "I'll get security to check the CCTV in the ambulance bay for a number plate." The linoleum squeaked as he turned on his heel. "Could take a while, but we should be able to chase him up."

———

Huian

It was taking too long. Huian wanted to scream. Didn't they know Mei couldn't wait? Didn't they know her little girl was fighting for breath? She had to go home. If she couldn't make the doctors understand, then why stay here? She was supposed to be looking after Mei for Lihua. She'd promised!

At the airport the day they'd left, Lihua had turned away, not wanting Mei to see her tears. Huian's daughter had sacrificed so much, missed so much, and what she had missed, Huian had gained: the weekends making steamed *bao* with Mei, the girl's sleeves rolled to her elbows and her nose dusted with rice flour; the way she pursed her lips when she painted the red dot on the top of the dumplings, so they could tell which ones were pork and which were chicken. And Mei would always eat the last one, the final sad little dumpling when there was not enough meat filling left in the bowl and barely enough rice dough to shape into a ball. Mei sang Disney songs in the shower, forgot to wipe the walls, and always used too many towels. At night she snored, a tiny hiccupping snuffle that made Huian smile.

Was Mei still sleeping?

Was she still *breathing*?

Huian gathered all her strength and flung her good arm across her body. She gasped. Someone was smashing the back of a meat cleaver on her skull. Ignoring the pain, she moved her foot under the sheet, shuffling her weight to the side of the bed. She gritted her teeth. Sweat dripped down her face and onto the pillow. She just needed to slide off the bed, that's all. Get her feet under her. Then she'd go home. A thought blossomed with the pain; they might even follow her…

Huian lurched sideways. She thudded to the floor, white bursts stabbing across her vision. The last thing she heard was someone shouting.

———

Andrea

While the patient was unconscious, Andrea booked the imaging suite to do a head scan, then entered the cubicle to swab the patient for COVID. The woman looked so tiny strapped to the bed. It was as if she'd shrunk since she'd been admitted.

He felt the tiniest twinge of guilt. So, they hadn't been able to get her informed consent before carrying out the tests; it was an emergency and they needed answers. Her condition was deteriorating. What were they supposed to do? Let the poor woman die on the floor while the translators got their act together? Well, they'd missed their opportunity. If they phoned in now, it'd be a bit of a one-sided conversation, given she was unconscious. Andrea was going off shift soon, but he'd left a message for the hospital's translation services to send someone up tomorrow. Assuming the woman woke up.

Andrea pulled the swab from the test kit and carefully inserted it in the woman's nasal cavity. That done, he popped the swab in a tube labelled with the patient number she'd been given when she'd arrived. He checked his watch. Fifteen minutes until the next batch of specimens were sent down to the medlab. If he was quick, he might make it. Still, he stopped to check the restraining straps before he left.

Why had she tried to get out of bed, anyway?

———

Huian

Huian became aware of the buzz of voices, the beep of machines.

Where was she? The hospital. Yes.

She opened her mouth to ask what day it was, what time, but she couldn't speak. Her chest hurt, her body and her shoulders shaking with the effort of breathing. She was dizzy, weak.

A soft voice, like Lihua's, spoke in her ear. Was her daughter here? No, the voice was Chinese, but not Lihua's. Her daughter was far away making money to send to Huian for her baby's education.

The baby! Mei was still at home alone. Huian had gone to get help. When was that? Yesterday? Or the day before? Huian's eyes flew open.

She screamed at the doctors. "My granddaughter needs help!" But her lungs were empty. What should have been a wail was merely a whisper.

Huian shuddered. Hands emerged from behind her head—someone holding a metal gun-thing. They pushed the tube down her throat. *No!* She had to tell them about Mei.

She gagged. Thrashed.

They had to listen! The baby was alone. She was sick.

Another voice. Hard. Insistent.

There was a prick in her arm.

Mei…

THE TOLL

Z.Z. Claybourne

The sharp click from pressing play on the tape recorder felt wrong in the forest's quietude. Outside, after a brief shower, drips from the roof counted the seconds of spool hiss.

She watched the rotation of the tape mechanism through the dark plastic rectangle.

Two more seconds of silence, then his voice.

"I've seen you feed. A bunch of times. You trust me that much? Catching and sniffing at the air that quick way you do. You that confident or is the plan to come for me? Nine nights I've seen you. When I hid behind a tree I imagined you saw me through the bark. Knew all I had to do was peer around the side and you'd be there, distant, standing with the moon behind you. Glowing eyes looking dead at me. You're a witch. You made me do this. All day I think about you, what you look like, what your name is. All the things like how your hair looks after you've been caught in the rain." The tape went quiet a moment. "Do you get caught in the rain? And then at night I search the woods, hoping to see a shadow or your quick form shooting between the trees, so soundless, so quiet…God, you're quiet! First time I saw you is the only time I've heard you make a sound. Terrified as I was, rifle in hand, paralyzed behind those bushes, you saw me and deliberately finished your feed, made that sound again, and left like a leopard. God, what the hell was that? It sounded like dying. Every night this month I've been out no matter what the weather. In the rain. In the fog. Do you understand? I'm only doing this because you let me. Nine times I've watched you and followed wherever you led.

Or tried to. I'm only doing this because I know you can't ignore it like you do me in the woods. I've got copies of this in safe places. And there's an attack dog here, and I sleep with my gun. I've covered my ass. Believe it. I disappear and people will know—"

The tall woman stopped the tape and ejected it. Long fingers closed around it, crushed the plastic rectangle, and dropped the pieces into the trash beside the old oak table. Rain started up again, hard now, with added wind, sheeting the window. She stood, stretched just for the sensation, and walked to the open door of the cabin where she leaned against the frame and watched water shatter on her porch. Just beyond it, the ground dotted into islands of mud. She closed her eyes and inhaled deeply. Her kind had always enjoyed the scent of forest rain.

She decided to take the player back to him in a bit, wrapped tight in plastic since he'd so thoughtfully provided machine along with the tape. In a few hours, the gray sky would go dark.

She imagined him asleep, rifle and dog patrolling his dreams to keep nightmares away. *Nice voice,* she thought. Dramatic flair. Verbose, as they usually were. Could've made a decent actor.

She went to her small, stove-less kitchen and opened the cupboard for her Jar of Life, a large teal jar made by a lovestruck missionary in nineteenth century Chokwe, who'd followed her to Franceville until she finally had to leave the country altogether. The jar contained packets of a milky, gelatinous substance. She punctured one with a tooth and squeezed its contents onto her tongue, the grimace instantaneous, the taste horrid, but it dulled the pains of transformation.

Then she bit into a lemon. It obliterated the stink of a taste. For something to unscrew her face, the rum she kept in the bottom cupboard.

———

The tall woman watched him cry.

He knelt on the ground, hands holding the black barrel pointed upward as if to shoot the moon. He shook. He bit his lower lip to keep it from trembling. The gutted carcass of his dog looked at him, its head impossibly twisted. He whimpered at it. "I'm sorry."

"Why'd you do it?" he put to her, knowing she was out there somewhere. "He was just a fuckin' dog. Why'd you kill the damn dog? Fucking bitch!" The dog always barked. It had stopped barking a few minutes ago, stopped on a dime. Silence roared. Silence yanked him from his dreams. He'd woken sweaty and afraid. All night he'd dreamed of the cassette, of why he wasn't out looking for her tonight...and the moment consciousness hit he *knew* it was her the same way he knew that the beast was female: she had made a connection with him (he was sure of it), had planted herself in too many of his fantasies and thoughts in this isolated forest. There were no other cabins for a ten-mile radius. Just him and her. He knew. He'd searched.

Searched a long time.

He immediately took up the gun.

His hands were clammy on the rifle stock as he crept out in underwear and slippers. He noticed the plastic-wrapped cassette player immediately, placed as it was just out of reach of the door's arc, water beads on the wrapping. She had been on his porch.

And then the dog at the side of the house, neck broken and partially eaten. He clapped a hand over his mouth. Vomit spilled from his fingers, some of it spotting the dog's carcass before he could turn. He whirled, taking his hand away, and vomited till his chest ached and the dry heaves cracked. When they passed, he flecked bits of food off his hand, then wiped the hand on the hip of his briefs. His eyes watered so much he couldn't see.

He plopped his butt to the squishy grass, made no move to clear his sight. "Why'd you do it?" He cursed her. He hated her. Fucking bitch. Time without feeling passed, minutes without thought or meaning, before he braced his hands near the tip of the rifle and got to his knees. Eventually he stood. Thirty minutes after that he wiped sweat from his forehead, leaving a grimy streak. He jabbed his shovel into the ground beside a mound of muddy dirt and left the fresh grave, stepping robotically: onto the porch, over the cassette player, closing the door.

All while she watched. And she knew that he knew—although in his mind the thought was forcefully blocked—that she was there, in the woods, moving with him, so smooth and quick and silent, watching his reactions. "Nine times…" The thought drew a lip above her canines. A fool turned familiarity into threats. Had he become so comfortable with what he thought was her, what she had *let* him witness his precious nine times, that he was entitled to her?

Nine meant nothing to her. She counted her days in centuries. She gave a low growl and left.

Thoughts of him were clear the following morning. He'd be in a state. Anger, fear, confusion, sorrow—a dangerous mixture. He would think of retaliation because he was a fool, then of flight because deep down she knew he wasn't suicidal enough to have made copies of the tape, thus actually endangering her so that she'd have no choice but to kill him.

He'd have to run. He needed a weapon against her. He'd get frantic. He'd dig up his evidence as soon as he fell out of bed, then be out of there and in his jeep for somebody—scientist, zookeeper, vet, anybody moderately intelligent enough to see that something was unusual in this death. They'd protect him.

As Paul threw clothes on, she yawned her way to her open door and rubbed her eyes.

Humidity greeted her. She loved it. She raised her arms full above and stretched herself toward the world before getting dressed. Jeaned (as he ran outside for the shovel, asking the dog to forgive him), bloused and shoed, she walked to her porch, closed the door, and made her way through the woods until she came to the little roundabout path that pretended to snake randomly through the trees. She paced herself to make the eight miles in ten minutes.

———————

Paul drove the shovel into the ground with the heel of his boot again, continuously muttering that none of this was his fault, pausing only when the sticky sweat clinging to his forehead slid too close to his eyes.

This wasn't how this was supposed to happen. He knew her secret.

That gave him power over her, didn't it? She was supposed to acknowledge that. She was! Not a single woman had said no to him when he'd worked in movies, not one.

He dug and dug. Halfway there.

While she *was* there.

He hadn't noticed her. She stepped on a twig for him. He shot erect.

There was no chance of him running.

The moment snapped him in half.

She was the most beautiful thing he'd ever seen.

Dear God in heaven, he wouldn't run. He could *want* to run all he wanted. His brain supplied any number of escapes…but actually attempting any of them was out of the question.

She approached him like a hiker seeking directions.

He thought of the shovel.

Her eyes fixed on his. They pierced skull and brain and exited the back of his mind. He stayed motionless as she came directly before him. A seizure of animal lust added to the fear. It made him realize that this was just a woman, a woman wearing a plaid shirt and faded jeans, staring at him, a woman with brown eyes and bangs of dark hair over her forehead, right here, right now, nothing more than a woman. One who was tall, but he was taller and bigger.

His grip tightened on the shovel.

Quietly, she glanced him up and down, even circled him, stepping on no more twigs. When she faced him again he noticed something different. Her right eyebrow was raised, like she was waiting for something.

For him to speak.

He swallowed hard. Sweat itched his back. He wanted so badly to swing that shovel then run like hell.

It took him a moment to realize that the garbled words he haltingly heard were his own.

"Please. No. No. I'm sorry. I swear, I didn't mean anything."

She didn't say anything. She made a hand motion for him to replace the soil. When he was done, she walked away. He followed.

When they reached her cabin his legs gave out.

She hoisted him up easily, then opened the door, standing aside. He stopped.

"Fighting rubber sharks is easy," she said.

He frowned.

"Schlock movie stuntman. Big out-of-court settlement. Blackballed out of the biz. No more glitz. Live in the woods and be a man."

Shit.

"You think I've never seen a movie? This isn't an enchanted forest. I step well out of its bounds. I recognized you."

He'd never gotten a full ten seconds of screen time.

She entered the cabin. He followed. She didn't close the door.

"I didn't…I didn't…I didn't mean anything with that tape. Swear to God. I lied anyway! I never made a copy, wouldn't send it to anybody. Never tell anybody!"

"And you planted the dead dog hoping it'd grow back? This is not one of your movies. You enjoy insulting me. That's too bad. Tell you right now, you won't survive the night."

His legs gave out again. On his knees, his sweaty fear assaulted her senses.

If he lost control of his bowels on her floor…

"Get up! Sit." He'd barely missed knocking into the rustic table and chair beside him. Her blue bottle sat atop it. "You enjoy the sound of your own voice too much."

"What are you going—"

"Don't ask questions, damn you!"

His dam broke. He had no way to hide it or his mortification, he just looked into her eyes like the frightened, whipped puppy he was.

A thick growl filled the room and chilled skin and blood. The warm urine felt like ice. He held his breath.

The growl stopped. Annoyed that he merely sat there looking at her with that ridiculously pained face, she snapped, "You see that door? It's hardly ever closed and not once has an *animal* come in here. Get back there and clean yourself off." Back there: a yellow door in a far corner of the cabin.

His thoughts looped while he walked: there was no moon; it was not night; she was just a woman, twenty-five, twenty-eight at the most; he was bigger than her; front door was open; no moon, no night, just a—

The loop broke the instant the bathroom door shut. It was a small bathroom, not much bigger than an outhouse with a tub. Out of sight he cried freely but made certain to choke off the noise. He turned the taps full on. The tub filled quickly. She hadn't said how long to take. He stripped and submerged till his knees stuck high above the low rim and his hair floated. After a few moments in the hot water his heart settled enough to allow him to lean back and close his eyes, to try to think.

Then he looked down at himself and saw the idiot rod pointing. Fear and lust triggered strange reactions. He viewed the erection as though it were something alien. It was oblivious to the situation; it was a fool. He forced a deep breath and allowed the water to warm him, to lift the grime and urine off, to provide him with the fantasy that she wasn't going to kill him. She'd given him a bath. It was quiet out there. She was thinking. Reevaluating him. Five full minutes he high-wired that tenuous thread, then she knocked on the door. She didn't say anything, just that single sharp, precise rap. He scooped water and rubbed grime off his face. Pulled the plug. Stepped out. Dried quickly. There was nothing to wear but the towel. A large red towel. Paul wrapped himself, then gathered his clothes and boots, and quietly exited.

"You wanna clean this up now?"

"Where's your—Do you have a mop?"

She pointed it out. He dropped the clothes by the table and quickly dabbed the spot. He worked at angles where his front wouldn't be seen for more than a glimpse. When finished he sat. He kept his hands against his lap.

"Boy. What did you think I would do, boy?"

He shifted.

"What do you know about me, Hollywood boy? I'll bet you're more ignorant than I credit."

"Are you going to kill me?"

She dismissed it with a wave. "It's early. How old are you?"

"Twenty-seven."

"Don't know much about sex, then. You think that little erection occupies me?"

She was looking directly at it. He pressed harder.

"Let the damn thing go!" She felt his heart jump from where she sat.

"You can't just murder me," he blurted. "Jesus, you'll be found when they look for me."

She unbuttoned her blouse.

He trailed the soft V of flesh. Her shirttails cleared the jeans.

She wished there was a moon visible, or the stars.

"You're not special, are you, Hollywood boy?"

"I'm just a guy."

"How many just guys like you? Just regular guys. How many?"

She caught a dart-like whiff of panic from him.

He studied her for reaction, hoping to see something. A smile. A softening. If she smiled, that would be good. He might live.

She didn't.

"The roads we take," she said. "You were dead when you decided I was prey." Here there be wolves. She took her jar from the table.

When she pulled out a packet, he stammered, "What's that?"

She swallowed, then went to retrieve a lemon from the sink counter. "We travel the roads; we pay the tolls." She stepped fully out of her clothing.

To his clogged ears it sounded like she said, "troll."

She changed in front of him. Silver fur, silver eyes. Claws like sickles. Sleek, tall, muscular, a thing made to be left alone, a thing to be watched only in silence.

If at all.

In silence and forgotten.

He tried running. She snatched him quickly back.

He wasn't worth eating, just a quick death.

That night, when her claws dug into his back—not viciously but efficiently: to pick him up, take him out of her home, and out of her life, back to be buried with his dog—the moon and stars were out. The rains had gone. She searched the interior of his cabin. Nothing of interest beyond other weapons and accumulated stuff.

She left his door wide open so animals could enter.

Then she went home, the pads of her feet making barely a sound on the forest floor.

ARISTOTLE'S LANTERN

Joanna Koch

In the opening sequence, we see the beat, the rush, the car crash. It reads as the end, but, for Adrasteia, it's the start of the shoot. In the jump-cut logic of the film, the last scene is when she shines. The curtain drops, and Adrasteia opens wide. Wide victim eyes. Where she is, she doesn't know. Dark place. Harpoon edges. Stink of fish meat. Adrasteia scrambles for a beacon, trawls inward for an unbroken line. She'll have flashbacks of how the men gathered, the sound of the ignition sputtering, the pervasive wetness. So much debris they fit inside of her. How soon after release the film stock starts to rot. In a few years, or seconds, it won't matter what they do to her body, because, in the long run, the body dies, and the soul forgets.

Aware after impact, diegetic dripping sounds in her field of vision. Hanging. The men in various corners. The nightmare knowledge that there is no way out. The giggling man, before he senses her presence. Close up on his work bench. Cut to Adrasteia's eyes. Precious prequel seconds in shadow. High contrast lights. Shaky camera. Clicking sounds. The moment to run lost. Her silent shock legitimizes a gore discourse with urban legends. When rough hands take her down, Adrasteia doesn't scream.

Frames shuffle like cards. The viewer feels disoriented, a kidnap victim when the hood comes off. Attrition subverts narrative lucidity due to incompetence or cinematic design. The result is that the viewer is forced to work harder to follow the shattered plot and is exhausted into submission. If they don't walk out in rage, they accept their passive stance and let the violence wash over them. Likewise, Adrasteia, in the role of her death-time, grinds downward from denial to grasping, from savior to grave. Her head seeks a hero, awash in nihilist disbelief. No way out. Nothing she's done to deserve this. Her fatal mistake was being born.

Pan to the giggling man. Rotted seafood texture of cinéma vérité. Car crash graphics. Homicide stock. Blurbs across Adrasteia's body, schoolgirl uniform ripped. Found footage warnings in red splatter letters. Life is cheap. Redemption is impossible. There will be no coming of age.

Jump cut to adult. Praying naked with a mouth full of razorblades, Adrasteia argues the minutiae of autonomy through restrained gestures. The set remains the same. The men haven't aged. She seeks to please her captors with a hospital mimesis counted out in five-four time. Scraping, she never weeps. Her posture, as defined by the surrounding wreckage of bodies, offends the viewer with a livelier set of fetishes.

Her involuntary desire to trust. The heart of a child. The light of silence bejeweling her tongue. A crack in the free-floating bone Adrasteia keeps latched. Backstory submerged in sequential dissonance, dark and silent as a severed head thrown into the sea.

Her silence is silver. It's X-acto-knife sharp, made of ingrown blades. The tightening collet of redacted lines pinches her mouth shut. Never tell. Don't bother to scream. Don't cry for help. The call is coming from inside your mouth.

Adolescent flash forward. Adrasteia was born for this scene. All her life, she thinks, or was taught to think, or began to think—when she started getting into character because there was no other way to turn except inward and deeper—she was meant to hold calisthenic ejaculations and recycled glass in full public view without complaint.

The soon-severed head of Adrasteia isn't empty, though it floats above her body in the film's aftermath. It's too soft-spoken for the average oracular snuff film fan to enjoy her radial cephalization. Adrasteia reads her own thoughts, forgotten prophecies sourced from external kicks in the teeth and unprocessed grief.

An intrusive voice-over speaks for the mute actress.

"The men are laughing at you. You have clots in your knees. You can't wait for your head to get cut off, yet you bargain for delays like a miser and take it up the blowhole, great and white. You'll regret it if you live to tell the tale."

Her silence is ship's brass. It oxidizes with the inconsistency of genital warts. When another missile erupts, Adrasteia colors it pink with froth from her saved saliva. From sores in her mouth that still bleed. What the men have done with her so far is nothing compared to what happens in the second and third films. The sequels bleach her horns faster than Adrasteia can shave off their weight. She remains inescapable.

It's a hoax, of course. The most basic critical analysis leaves no question in the viewer's mind that Adrasteia doesn't survive.

Wide shot. One man collapses like a hangover. One is worn out, one hiding, and another prepares fresh handfuls of razorblades extracted from last year's candy. He'll use the slender devices to compromise the nemeses inside Adrasteia's body. There's a consensus among the men that she needs new teeth.

The amateur operation isn't meant to cure her ordeal or enhance longevity. It's purely for fun. By the time it's over, the internal pain of calculated edges proves every motion of her pelvis a slice.

Her role requires consent, and the call to action catches her off-kilter. With the next scene on deck, the camera is sinking, sliding. The set rests on salts, on channeled lungs, and keening waters. Speak no more of your missing daughters. Adrasteia reaches underside in agony according to the implicit script. She's retracted by habit. Jailbait Gehenna constant, with movable spines. The men laugh at the sight of her susceptible decline.

The viewer can't tell when the scene happens, or how old Adrasteia is meant to be, due to the obfuscation of blood. Other than the notorious coda, this scene is a favorite among fans. Adrasteia fingers herself and loses another digit. One man hoots, one threatens death if she stops, and another martyrs an existence fragrant with lost children, for he himself is lost. Where he spills his sperm, hopes die.

Adrasteia's thumb pops off. Her acting is strained and desperate, trying the patience of her co-stars. Perhaps it's the contrast between agonized facial contortions and her muteness that creates an accidental comic effect, thus alienating the viewer's sympathies. The men engage in casual debate, trying to decide if it's still fisting when all that's left of her hand is a bloody nub.

The enticement of decay is too pungent to dismiss as mere crisis. The men circle Adrasteia, rattling dice. Wreaths of cilia extend like seaweed from her ears, exaggerating every sound. She can count how long she's been here by measuring the distance the fine hairs travel towards surface or solace. Silky woven ropes bind her head in stillness, aggravated by anaphylactic sex. The old familiar voice-over is near null, near prophet.

"The getaway car crashed before you were conceived as a spark. You will not escape the last scene alive. Where invertebrates fear to tread…well, you know the rest. Cozy up to a gaffer if you want more light."

The intrusive narration further distances the viewer from the immediacy of the extended torture scene, placing them outside a dirty fish tank peering in through layers of algae. This approach wears down the viewer's strained gaze and degrades the eye by means of squalid production values and haphazard editorial choices less amateur than malicious. If art gives, this takes.

The viewer feels detached, dirty, and used. It's all her fault. Just look at that bitch groveling under the pointed indifference of the camera lens. Listen to her silence. The sound of a body in distress. The harbinger of irreparable damage to come. Adrasteia shrinks audibly from the knife-like rays strobing her throat in close-up.

Adrasteia is inevitable, like some underwater nun. Her vow of silence is chlamydial. Its side effect is time travel. Adrasteia everywhere: in the fish tank, in the viewer's lap, in the critic's eye. Her absence from her body stinks up the set. The viewer feels both disgusted and aroused by the growing odor. The giggling man winks at the fourth wall. Complicit critics spread her scent through nasal telepathy. The men and their understudies develop a taste for rare bacteria endemic to Adrasteia's injuries. The more disease they squeeze out of her, the greater their thieves' delight.

They dance raucously around the victim and sing a shanty, hooked elbows a-circling. Adrasteia is disarmed by the lack of continuity. How the hell is she supposed to detonate? Her role is already challenging enough. The self she plays in opposition to her deeper oceanic death necessitates escape by preventing its possibility. The men surround her, singing, stomping out a heartbeat. The words are runoff gibberish. A scrabbling coral bounces on each syllable where the subtitles invade the screen.

The viewer prays along. Nudity is encouraged.

Adrasteia martyr. Adrasteia fruit cup. Adrasteia daughter of no one. Adrasteia of the silted horde, miniscule in sea kelp. Adrasteia unheard of, zero in being, in gift of verticality, in binding with drowned thresholds, in complex spasms of water, in hidden light, in manifest light, under a shield that is not a storm. Adrasteia chewing through calcareous luminescence, bidden by endless becoming.

The giggling man chants, clothed in someone else's skin. Adrasteia extrudes her new teeth in the shape of a key. She hides it from her captors under the sluggish pinprick of her tongue. The problem with a plot about kids recovering from being sex trafficked is that there are no kids, only traffic. Pedestrians win you ten points apiece. Stealing a police car gets you five stars. Looting boosts health. If Adrasteia breaks character and whispers in the policeman's ear that she's been kidnapped, he will not hear her. She lacks the cognitive framework to formulate the lines in the correct semantic sequence.

Adrasteia passes the policeman, leaking fluids from her severed neck. The cop is as much help as a preacher, less than a towel. Too much shame for sunlight. Too much sound for a spliced journey. Her lips split, unsure if their restructured shape is the result of a shipwreck or a car crash, unsure how to emit an explanation of what's wrong with the conceptual arc of this disordered plot. After all, she's a child, not a fucking script doctor. The cop retches away in disgust. The viewer suppresses a guilty laugh.

Adrasteia's head drifts to the bottom of a sea with no floor, plunging to unending depths. Her hair spins in slow motion, circling her head like a nest. Her eyes remain wide. A single bubble escapes her razor-cropped mouth and takes the opposite path to the surface.

Top equals darkness. Silence equals death. The viewer offers patronizing advice, hand on Adrasteia's thigh, hiding under the camouflage of the giggling man's skin. "Never trust the cops. They'll haul you in and take your money. Relax. Be yourself."

Short of being allowed to take a shower, Adrasteia won't experience the privacy required to learn to act natural and be herself, especially with a stranger's hand stroking her thigh. Who her self is supposed to be depends on an underground world where people are treated like meat and you walk through your life as if none of this is happening, as if your children are safe. The problem with making a snuff film is that there's only one way it can end. Pornography in general suffers from a similar ritualistic crux. Adrasteia is running out of options while you watch the film in your comfortable chair as if none of this is real, as if none of this is your problem.

The viewer communicates arousal by fondling a proxy. The giggling man stands atop the shipwrecked pyramid of bodies mangled after the impact of the first sequence. His dominance is alluring to the audience. His crotch reeks of motor oil. He rumbles like a balloon, which is to say, he squeaks.

The narrative arc swings back and forth through time with absurd abandon. Adrasteia's oracular constriction reads as deliberate ignorance, unforgivable in a sacrificial hostage. The men round up more razorblades to hollow out the rest of her and scrape her carapace clean. The soaked terrain provides a palisade where Adrasteia is forced to ride.

Floating at the surface of the set with barely enough water to breathe, Adrasteia eyes the ignition between slashes of the giggling man's camera moves. The wrecked vehicle steams. Her tongue licks her heated key. Adrasteia wishes herself small enough to squeeze into the space between lapsed frames. In the flicker of incandescent bulb knives, she could blink out and be gone.

Flawed, she corrupts each darting chance with doubt. The location isn't familiar, so Adrasteia doesn't know where to exit the set. She tries parsing it out through the oppressive narration, unheard like a murmur on her shell. Statements carved in blood tattoos bore deeper as they fade. A show of ownership internalized. Proof of the rumor mill hangs like a stone piercing her genital plate. Every suggestion makes cracks. Silent chemical signals. Death by a thousand cuts.

The giggling man snatches the key Adrasteia formed out of her anatomy. Adds it to his toolbox. It's never seen again.

Voice-over in red.

"There's no point in running anyway because shit happens and then you die. Or shit gets real, and then you live. The key is that it's all shit."

Her tongue like a lantern, silent, lighted for fog. Divinatory shapes expelled, read fast like hot intestines. Adrasteia makes prophecy under the surface of its prongs, without protest. She grows a mastectomy long enough to blur through an underground glen and blot out all the fronds curling in the underwater crevasse. Deeper into the journey, swallowing a sea cave hollowed out in steel where hide her stablemates, Adrasteia reaches for fattened tankers rolling on the ocean floor. Sisters in poison, slender at sea level, whispering curses of sea urchins.

"You are your body. You cannot escape."

As foreshadowed in the opening moments, Adrasteia shudders, ageless, elegiac, and unclothed. Her heart beats loud and wet like Leviathan pounding the tides. Slithering strokes like sneaking footsteps swath an endless interim with sheets of panic pulled tight. In this place, where she's sharpened by scraping, the light itself is darkness. Adrasteia glows, shaved thin enough to allow light through, strong enough to keep the air out. Her dim aquatic hole where the dead go to hide.

The cave walls leak like a syphilitic prick. Her voice-over sisters spit bones, sticky tendrils, eruptions of salt. "It's best to stay intoxicated. There is a weakness you exude that attracts abuse. Here, try one of these before they start in on you again."

Adrasteia reasonably concludes that this is all her fault. She needs to cauterize her sloppy orgasm or risk greater humiliation. The deep sea swaddles her erotically. The heart of a child snuff film is an exploration of the death of God. The giggling man has prepared an inventory of tools for the denouement. The special edition disc set comes with a list of his devices and how he uses them in each clip. Commentators speculate that he's the one talking when the viewer next listens in greedily on Adrasteia's secret voice.

"You are not a ghost, even when you try to be."

The disjointed narration struggles to impose theatrical order in the absence of plot continuity. Questions remain around the origin of the text.

"This nightmare is brought to you by assembly required."

"You can't speak. You can't escape."

The voice-over fails to intensify the viewer's arousal. Alienation from the victim is subverted by the awkward use of second person verb tense. The voice-over fails on all fronts.

"There are fissures in the—look, just trust me on this, okay? There are fissures, ha ha, and fishers of men. You are not a stone, no matter how fast you sink. Pay attention. You will remember all of this, whether you live or not."

The giggling man is taking Adrasteia apart one razorblade at a time. The intense pleasure of this experience is more confusing to her than the gnawing fear that things can only get worse. She'd hate her body for its erotic response if she believed it was still alive. Adrasteia is glad that she was never born, so she has nothing to remember. She won't have to figure out what to say regarding her role in the corruption of minors when the interviewer for the special features accuses her of complicity as an adult.

Adrasteia chooses silence. Silence is an absence of light.

When he's done deconstructing, Adrasteia allows the giggling man to rebuild her because there's no one else left. There never was. The wet, greasy muscles of the people posing like mannequins in the position of a car crash or shipwreck have failed to successfully ignite. The giggling man like a charioteer rides loud and golden above. He gestures in bone. Gestures in spine. Gestures in calcium carbonate. Makes a mess of everyone's skin. Adrasteia's new skeleton is made of razorblades and tempered hornlight. Broken windshield wipers beat a festive, irregular dirge. Adrasteia feels nostalgia. She was once a girl with a heartbeat.

Here she goes. It's time. Here's where Adrasteia makes her entrance on the set, but really, the set comes to her, as the earth hurls dirt at the windshield, and the ocean rushes in to swallow her face. Entertainment is the priority in her long-delayed execution, and it's hard to say a safe word with a mouth made of salt. Adrasteia is silence. Silence is ambergris.

The giggling man goes quiet. Adrasteia is wet. She listens for sirens but help never comes. The mermaids are strangled and hung up like meat. Her escape efforts drown. The car won't start. The set is closed. The giggling man is ready. She's a leak he can fix.

Adrasteia, in character, refuses to speak. The film is silent. Nudity blares. Her tongue like a lantern; prayer is silent. It's Adrasteia's moment to turn over and ignite. The clicking of cameras. Of posthumous tools. Of glassy events. Of oracular lamps. Of noduled tests. Of untapped venom. Of pentamerous teeth. Of steel, of coral, of underground mountains. Of holes.

The room has no windows. The set has no lights. The room is outside.

The film is a black screen with no sound. When the men find what's inside, they leave Adrasteia for dead. Her last words flash on the screen. She can't hear them because the film is silent. She can't hear them because they were never said.

Her tongue like a lamp ruled by darkness. Journeying inward, where feeling is the opposite of being. Of those beings ruled by matter, doomed to skin. Her inexpert beheading is a finite event from which she will recover. The soul never forgets. This light, in her coming, beats and comes again. The beat is with Adrasteia. Her light walks upon the face of the deep.

The light flattened on a black screen. The light locked in a basement. The light kidnapped and fucked hard and taken to Denny's for breakfast. The light grown indifferent. The light doesn't know how to save us. It can only give us more interesting STDs. The light in her mouth like a virus, inflamed by the sound of the beat.

Adrasteia, ancient, recalling a film that never was seen. The viewer will root for the maniac. while she, the silent final girl, the final light, swims in black circles around the mass death of a coral reef. Submerged, she'll live more than one hundred years. Regenerating lost and damaged parts, replacing fingers and spines, vibrating with the slow refusal of heroic life, the underwater footage of her famed alternate ending has survived.

In the restored coda, the shell's decoration of scars beautifies a body discarded as wreckage. Long thought extinct, the siren defies environmental disaster. The viewer sighs, and whether this sound signifies disappointment or relief is the test of their entrance into the myth.

Extending this lantern like hope over death, Adrasteia opens the spiny gates of her complex, reborn orifice. In vocalizations vulnerable across unknown regions of distress, in sharing the scrape of sentiment times zero times five, the eleven worlds birthed from the carcass of Adrasteia come alive too sharp to stay focused for more than a single eon. The viewer's screen is bleached with blackness. The child's last mistake is being born. Adrasteia argues, spewing kelp and sperm and salty bones. On the set, the light is darkness. Inside, there is no exit. Outside, above the water's surface, the sound of traffic is louder than God.

BAD GREEN, QUIET BLACK

Gabino Iglesias

Pestalotiopsis microspora. The name rang a bell. Roberto tuned out for a second. Dr. Dahlby's words became unintelligible sound in the background even though the man was speaking only a few feet away from his face. Then it all came back with the speed of rushing water.

He'd read the article about six months before in *Applied and Environmental Microbiology.* Although he recalled the findings, the names of those responsible for the study evaded him. *Pestalotiopsis microspora* was a fungus found in Ecuador by a team of researchers from Yale. The fungus could eat polymer polyester polyurethane via a process called bioremediation. The now nameless researchers had isolated the enzyme that allowed the fungus to break down plastics. If Roberto recalled correctly, the next step would be to mass-produce the voracious fungus and then unleash the powers of bioremediation on landfills. It was the kind of finding that made the news for about three seconds and then vanished except for obscure academic journals.

Roberto came back to the conversation in time to realize he'd missed the most crucial part of it.

"And that's why we need you to start working on this project, Roberto," said Dr. Dalhby. "I know how much time you've invested researching the Giant Polypore mutation, but I'm asking you to put your time and effort into this as a personal favor. If we don't give the feds a satisfactory report and convince them we have this under control, they're going to turn everything over to the Department of Health or the CDC. If they do, those guys will waltz in here and put a stop to everything we're working on right now until they can figure out exactly what happened to Dr. Mayorga and his daughter. Considering Mayorga was taking work home and never brought in the samples he acquired during his trips to Ecuador, you can bet they'll also get on our case about safety protocols. Do you see how the repercussions become exponentially worse if we don't take care of this now?"

"I understand, ma'am," replied Roberto. "I really don't know much about whatever Dr. Mayorga was working on." For a man who was more or less completely lost, Roberto thought he had framed the question in a way that made him seem only curious.

In reply, Dr. Dalhby grabbed a yellow folder that was sitting next to her phone and placed it on the desk in front of Roberto. Her mouth was a tight line that spoke volumes about how much she hated sharing information.

"Everything we know is in there," she said. "We also talked to the police and they're letting you into Dr. Mayorga's home after tomorrow. They only glanced at his papers and I'm sure they had no idea what they were reading. The detective in charge assured me they didn't remove anything. Apparently, they don't think there was any foul play. They're convinced Mayorga breathed in something that affected him on a neurological level, so they only took a cursory look at his home lab and sealed it off. That means his papers are still there, along with whatever he was working on. I hope his notes enlighten you. We need you to put an end to this quickly and quietly. If you ask me, he was overworked and his wiring simply short-circuited. Anyway, just remember you have to keep this quiet. Word of it gets out, you'll never work here or in any other lab ever again, so you can forget about sponsorship to stay in the country."

Roberto wanted to know more. The rumors in the hall were so awful they couldn't be entirely made up unless whoever started them had a Stephen King-level imagination. Considering Dr. Dalhby's attitude, it was clear the smart thing to do would be to take the folder and read its contents instead of asking anything else. The only thing he absolutely had to ask was about his current research.

"I'll try my best, Dr. Dalhby. Do you think when I'm done I can jump back on the Polypore mutation research? I fear the consequences will be disastrous if we don't—"

"—As soon as you figure out what Mayorga was working on and put together a report that tells the authorities everything's fine, you can go back to saving the trees, Roberto." This was said with a condescending smile and a nod. Roberto knew the nod well. It meant the conversation was over.

Roberto looked at the doctor sitting across from him and wondered how long it would take him to satisfy her. He wanted to flip through the folder, but there would be time for that later. Instead of looking at it, Roberto used the folder to wave his goodbye. A second later he was out of the chair and exiting Dr. Dalhby's office into the brightly lit hallway. Ahead, the door to his lab was open. He knew his place was in there, working on his latest research, a strange mutation of the Giant Polypore fungus.

Known scientifically as *Meripilus Giganteus*, the Giant Polypore fungus had long been known to be a problem for Beech trees. Once the fungus latched on to the root of a tree, rot would quickly follow. This turned affected trees into dangerous giants that could fall on someone with the help of a gust of wind. In the last year, *Meripilus Giganteous* had mutated. A ranch owner in Montana had seen four Ponderosa Pines come crashing down on his property in one week. The man's wife happened to be a professor in the College of Agriculture at Montana State University. She made a few calls and the problem landed in Roberto's lap. His PhD in Plant Pathology from Cornell made Dr. Dalhby throw anything that had to do with plants his way.

Roberto sat at his desk and opened the folder. He craved coffee, but his curiosity about Mayorga's death was a more powerful draw.

The first few pages were Dr. Rafael Mayorga's vita. Its thickness was impressive. The folder also contained printed articles and interviews with the doctor, unquestionably one of the top microbiologists of his generation. It was stuff Roberto had read or heard about before.

The last page was a note from the police. It stated that no further information could be provided about the ongoing investigation regarding the death of Mayorga. The note made it clear that Dawson Research, the company Roberto worked for, was welcome to send one of its own to look into the deceased doctor's home lab. There was a small card with a cell phone number. Underneath it was a name scrawled in the same tight cursive: Paul Wheeler. Roberto would have to call him to set up a time for them to meet. The detective would grant him access to Mayorga's home and lab. He decided to get that cup of coffee and call after.

————

The sun was high and there were no clouds in the sky when Roberto parked on the curb in front of Mayorga's home. The front of the house was split in half by a big chimney and decorative half-timbering gave the two-floor Tudor a look that danced between Medieval and creepy.

A man that Roberto took to be Paul Wheeler was standing by the door even though their meeting was not scheduled for another ten minutes. Roberto got out of the car, locked it, and approached him.

Wheeler had an angular face with a five o'clock shadow and a receding hairline. He wore a blue polo shirt that was a bit tight across his broad shoulders. Roberto said hello to the detective and stuck his hand out. Wheeler took the proffered hand and gave it a few hard, slow shakes.

"You Roberto?" asked Wheeler.

"Yes, sir. Detective Wheeler, right?"

"Call me Paul."

Letting go of Roberto's hand, Wheeler turned toward the door and pulled a set of keys out his right front pocket.

"Everyone that had to be in here has already come and gone. That's why we gave you guys access. We know Mayorga recently went to Ecuador and a lot of people would breathe easier if we knew that he simply went off his trolley and that his death and that of his daughter had nothing to do with anything he brought back from his trip. You familiar with his work?"

The detective had opened the door while he talked. Both men were now standing in Mayorga's living room. The scant furniture and lack of decorations on the walls confirmed what Roberto had already supposed: Mayorga had been a man for whom work always came first. Divorced almost as soon as his daughter was born, Mayorga had basically done nothing but work for most of his life. In a way, he was like every other immigrant.

"Mayorga was a microbiologist," said Roberto. "Lately, he had become obsessed with some of the properties of *Pestalotiopsis microspora,* a fungus that can eat plastic. He took a trip to Ecuador as soon as the findings about this new discovery came out. He spent a few weeks with the Huaorani, a semi-nomadic tribe living in the Amazonian rainforest. Mayorga considered their shamans eminences in all things horticultural. My guess is he was interested in how some of these fungi interact with other microorganisms in different scenarios in the real world."

The detective's eyes had glazed over. The man had probably expected something darker when it came to what Mayorga did with his life and the reasons for his trip. He stopped talking. It was always about silence. When his professors made him do all the work and then put their names first on his research papers, he had to stay silent and be grateful. When they offered him a job doing the same thing his friend Sebastian Cohen did for half the pay, he had to stay silent and be grateful. When folks talked about his accent instead of his research, he had to stay silent. When they sent him on bullshit errands like this, he had to stay silent. He was tired of silence.

"You think there's even a slight possibility that something he brought back from that rainforest could've made him crazy? You never know what's in those fucking godforsaken places. They should burn them all to the ground, you ask me. Nothing but wild people stuck in the stone age and weird diseases out there."

The question didn't take Roberto by surprise, but the casual racism did. Despite a lifetime of encountering it, it still shocked him. For all the wild theories and stories, he still didn't know exactly how Mayorga had died. He decided to try to find out more.

"To be honest, I might be able to answer your question if I knew a bit more about how he died. The file they gave me didn't say much."

Wheeler looked at him for ten seconds before replying.

"That information hasn't been given out to anyone. The media would have a party if we gave them the details. If I tell you and something leaks out to the press, I'll come looking for you. Am I making myself clear?"

The threat was not lost on Roberto. Since he had no plans to talk to any reporters, and anything Wheeler told him could possibly help him get through this and write the report sooner, he assured the detective the information was safe with him. His business, Roberto explained, was with whatever was in Mayorga's lab. Silence, again, was part of the deal.

"Mayorga was found in his lab with his daughter, Sonia Mayorga," explained Wheeler. "We assume he was showing her something he found interesting. According to the mother, the teenager spent odd weekends with his father and shared an interest for his work. It appears Mayorga came at her from behind and stabbed her three times in the neck with a pen. With his daughter bleeding to death on the floor, Mayorga tried to start a fire in the trash bin. He then used the same pen he'd killed his daughter with to gouge his eyes out and then stab himself in the carotid artery. He bled to death blind and probably thinking his fire was a success. Since there was very little paper in the bin, the fire puttered out. The cleaning lady found the bodies the next morning."

The image of Dr. Mayorga stabbing himself in the neck with a pen after gouging out his own eyes made Roberto feel woozy. Not one word of what Wheeler had said made any sense.

"I...nothing he brought back from the Amazonian rainforest could've possibly made him do that."

"That's good to know," said Wheeler. "I'm ready to read a report by you saying it's all clear so we can send a cleaning team in here and close this case. However, you have to understand that we're a bit worried. We're talking about a respectable, educated man here, not your run of the mill wet— construction worker. Something had to be wrong with him for him to kill his own daughter, you know? We usually don't run into murder-suicides where the perpetrator gouges his fucking eyes out before killing himself. We've interviewed anyone and everyone who could give us information about Mayorga, and everyone was just as incredulous and surprised as you. Mayorga wasn't the type to do something like this. The fact that it all went down in his lab makes us worried that there might be something in there capable of affecting people in a similar way."

A low buzz reached Roberto's ears. Wheeler pulled a cell phone out of his back pocket and slid his finger across the screen. A few monosyllabic answers later, the detective ended the call and looked at him.

"I gotta get out of here," Wheeler said, handing Roberto a set of keys. "When you're done, either drop these at the station or give me a call. If I'm nearby, I'll swing by and pick them up." Roberto grabbed the keys and thanked the detective. "No problem. Hope you can find something that helps us put this thing to rest."

Wheeler turned around and walked out the door. Roberto followed him. While the detective drove away, Roberto opened his car and picked up the box of gloves and the disposable mask he'd brought from his lab.

Although the sun was still as bright as when Roberto had gotten there a few minutes earlier, now he turned to look at the empty house behind him and an icy finger ran down his back. As he walked to the door again, the image of Mayorga driving a bloodied pen through his neck came back to him. The icy finger ran up Roberto's back and wrapped itself around the nape of his neck.

———

The lab was easy to find. As soon as Roberto reached the second floor, he saw the door at the end of the hallway was crisscrossed with yellow tape that read "POLICE LINE DO NOT CROSS." Wheeler had said nothing about which key opened the lab, so Roberto tried four before finding the right one. He used the same key to cut through the yellow tape.

The sight on the other side of the lab's door was something no one could have prepared him for. The room was big and there were three stainless steel tables pushed against the left wall. To the right, a large metal desk with a Formica top— that seemed to have been pulled from a government office in the 70's— held a microscope and some folders. In the back, four wall cabinets stacked on top of each other and a fridge completed the lab. The tables, the floor around them, and the entire wall behind them were covered in dark green fungi. Whatever Mayorga had been working on was now covered in something that looked like green mold gone wild.

Considering Mayorga's death had only taken place six days before and that the team of investigators had been there for two days, the growth Roberto was looking at had happened in about three or four days. That was impossible. He walked over to the desk and took a seat. He didn't have to rummage around too much to find what he was looking for. Mayorga was a very organized man and the only two folders on his desk had to do with his most current research.

Roberto opened the first folder and started reading the first sheet. He was surprised to see it was written in Spanish. He knew Mayorga was Ecuadorian, but scientists are usually forced to work in English if they do their research in the US. As Roberto soon learned, Mayorga also spoke Huaorani and a bit of Qechua as well. The notes seemed to be Spanish translations of conversations with the Huaorani people and other folks he met during his travels in Ecuador.

While looking for *Pestalotiopsis microspora*, Mayorga had run into a different fungus. When he asked the Huaorani shaman about it, he learned the natives avoided the green fungi at all cost and called it "bad green" in their native tongue. The shaman explained that those who listened to the sound of the bad green would go crazy and take their own life. The fungus was considered an evil spirit and the Huaorani refused to camp in places where it could be found growing.

According to the notes, touching the fungus caused people to have horrible hallucinations. Tribe members who had touched it were always found dead.

Roberto read through the rest of the first folder. It was mostly translated conversations from the trip, theories about how the *Pestalotiopsis microspora* had developed an enzyme that could process chemicals not naturally found in its habitat and some observations about how the Huaroani produced some of the most plague-resistant manioc in the world by constantly changing the soil in which they planted and staying away from monocultures.

The notes were interesting, but none of it helped Roberto much.

The second folder, however, turned out to contain exactly what he was looking for. Mayorga had subjected his samples to a plethora of tests and his notes recorded the way the fungi reacted. He pulled out a sheet and read it. Mayorga had either lost his mind or this was the strangest fungus in the world. The samples showed no reaction to water or heat, something that was unheard of. Likewise, the samples ate through organic and non-organic matter at the same speed. On the third day, Mayorga had walked into the lab to find that the fungi had eaten through their respective Petri dishes and were beginning to corrode the stainless-steel table. That meant the fungi were somehow chloridic in nature, which was also unheard of. Mayorga had reported his findings. According to his notes, higher ups at Dawson Research had told him to keep it quiet until he could find at least two ways of monetizing the fungus's bizarre properties.

Not willing to trust the notes of a man that had killed his daughter and then plucked out his own eyes, Roberto got up and walked over to the fungi-covered table. As he approached, a low hum stopped him in his tracks. At first, he thought the sound was coming from the fridge, but turning his head, he realized it came from the table. He took another step. The hum got louder. He looked at the table and thought he saw movement. It looked as if a small snake had moved underneath the blanket of fuzzy green.

His mind was obviously playing tricks on him. Roberto walked back and sat down. He picked up Mayorga's notes and started going over them again. The more he read, the crazier Mayorga's claims became. The microbiologist wrote he thought the fungus on his table was making a sound. After a few more lines, the writing became incoherent babble.

I touched the samples, read the page in Roberto's hand. *Something happened and I woke up to Sonia shaking me. Wanted to know if there was anything left of the Petri dishes. Now it's inside me. I've seen what's to come. I don't want us to be here when it happens. The shaman was right. THE SHAMAN WAS RIGHT!*

Like someone waking from a deep sleep on a plane and noticing the sound of the engines for the first time, Roberto realized the hum was gone, replaced by a low sound that alternated slightly in pitch. He focused on the sound. It wasn't music, but it had a rhythm to it. As a plant pathologist, Roberto knew some plants were capable of amazing things, but emitting a rhythmic sound was completely new to him. Maybe finding something so incredible had driven Mayorga crazy.

Leaving the notes behind, Roberto walked back to the tables. This time, he kept on walking even when the sound became louder at his approach. Now there appeared to be multiple snakes moving under the green blanket. He thought about the gloves, but he had left them outside the door when he was cutting the police tape. Before he could catch himself, Roberto reached out and ran his finger across the green blanket of fungi. It felt incredibly cold. Then a shock rocked his body and forced him to close his eyes.

The first sensation was strange, as if someone was trying to stretch his skull. The sound coming from the fungi became an unbearable cacophony of screams and unintelligible blabber. A flash of light blinded him and then the dense vegetation of the Amazonian rainforest was all around him. He could hear strange voices coming from everywhere at once; voices he knew couldn't come from human voice boxes. Then he saw a naked child approach. The kid opened his mouth to the sky and used his fingers to claw at his neck until blood gushed out in heavy spurts and ran down his chest. The flash came again and he saw the room he was in now. He saw Mayorga's body on the floor. There were ragged dark holes where his eyes were supposed to be. The blinding white light pulsed again. His perspective changed to that of someone looking up from the floor. Two hooded figures were standing over him. Their faces were dark and reptilian in nature. A second later he was looking into the face of one of those things. In the lifeless black eyes that stared back at him from the reptilian face, Roberto saw himself. He had become one of those creatures. Behind the thing in front of him, the outline of two monolithic structures rose into a heavy grey fog. The white light flashed again and he opened his eyes.

The floor felt cold against his cheek. When he raised himself up,

Roberto realized he had been lying on top of the fungi. The coldness climbed up his hands. He brought them up to his face and saw green sludge penetrating his skin. With his eyes wide open and frozen into inaction by fear, he watched as the last of the green fluid disappeared inside him. The inhuman voices he had heard when he was hallucinating came back even louder.

Roberto lowered his hands and stood up. He had to get out of there. He had to tell everyone about this. They had to contain this thing. Whoever tried to silence Mayorga should pay. Whoever tried to silence *him* now would find a very different Roberto, one no longer willing to keep his mouth shut to keep everyone else happy.

Roberto shook his head and took a step. Something was wrong with his legs. Maybe he had injured himself during the fall. His feet felt rubbery. Roberto looked down at his hands and forearms. Green spots covered his skin and a bulbous growth was pulsating near his left thumb. He was infected with something. Deep inside him, he knew the visions he had been shown accurately depicted fractions of the past as well as the future. He had to call Wheeler and let him know what has happening. Mayorga had the right idea: burn the house to the ground. He looked around for something to start a fire with. The green fungi now covered almost every surface of the room. The hum reached his ears and muddled his thoughts. Fire, he thought again. The kitchen was his only option. Stumbling around on wobbly legs, Roberto made his way downstairs.

Mayorga owned an electric stove. Roberto knew there had to be at least some matches in one of the drawers. When he reached for the first drawer, he noticed the tips of his fingers had flattened considerably and were becoming rounder. The skin on his arms was now mostly green. The strange voices in his head were becoming louder and his right leg twitched as if independent from his body. He pulled the drawer open. It contained only cutlery. A sudden movement came again. His leg was trying to move on its own. Roberto reached down to pull his pant leg up and the leg jerked back by itself, forcing him to topple forward and bump his head against a cabinet door.

There was some feeling still in his left leg and arms, but it was quickly fading as the blabbering and humming in his skull kept its steady crescendo. He wanted it to stay quiet, to obey the way he had obeyed everyone when they told him to stay quiet, but the sound refused.

The research came back on its own, breaking through Roberto's fear and desperation and stunning him into momentary inaction with its implications.

Ophiocordyceps unilateralis. It had been found in the Zona da Mata area in south-eastern Brazil a few months before *Pestalotiopsis microspora.* The news jumped all over it with crazy headlines because the story was too juicy to pass up. Scientists had discovered an entire family of fungi that could control ants by releasing chemicals into their brains after the ants came in contact with the fungi's spores. Once infected, ants would leave the nest, bite into a leaf and die in that position. The fungus inside each ant would then sprout a spore-bearing stalk out of the back of the neck of the dead ant and release its spores.

Roberto knew he was experiencing something similar. This fungus, however, acted much faster and was obviously only the beginning of a bigger, smarter life form. Suddenly, his legs started turning toward the door. Roberto understood the same thing Mayorga had. Mayorga had touched the fungi and become infected. So had Sonia. If he allowed this thing to fully take control of his body and walk out of the house, his death would only be the beginning of the end.

He tried to reach for his cell phone to call Wheeler, but his right arm remained dangling uselessly by his side. His own body was betraying him, forcing him to stay silent when it mattered most. Robert screamed. Whatever was inside him was acting quickly. All the scientific knowledge packed in his brain told him there was only one way to get rid of a parasite that had already taken over its host. Without another thought, the plant pathologist used his left hand to reach into the drawer in front of him. The knife had a serrated edge. Roberto closed his eyes and thought of his grandmother, who'd always told him to do the right thing regardless of the consequences. Roberto felt a pull and then heard his flesh rip open as he dragged the knife across his neck. There was no pain. His hands were no longer his, so he didn't bring them up to stop the blood spraying from his slashed flesh.

In the back of his mind, even over the cacophony of inhuman voices, Roberto knew that was a good thing. Then the voices began to ebb away as the kitchen around him became dimmer. A thought popped into his head like a light breaking through a cloudy sky: he hadn't found the damn matches. He tried to scream, but the sound caught in his throat. Then that silence swallowed him as the world turned green and then faded to a quiet black.

WHY WE KEEP EXPLODING

Hailey Piper

JUST A JOKE

The first girl explodes on the final evening of orientation weekend.

Allison Greer, Sutton University freshman, joins us in the dining hall, where all levels of college kids pack the inside, clacking dishes and loud voices bounding off every surface. Beneath that cacophony, no freshman would fear silence.

The boys who join us at our table are upperclassmen. They forego hoodies and torn jeans for stiff button-downs and slacks, like they have job interviews scheduled after dinner. Juniors? I can't say for sure.

The tallest, a blond boy with razor-straight teeth and a narrow face, sits across from Allison. I can't make out their conversation through the noise, but he points repeatedly to a cup of yellow liquid, likely beer, and then taps a penny on the tabletop, and I understand this is some kind of challenge.

She tells him she doesn't like games. When he doesn't let up, she curses him and throws her glass of fountain soda into his face.

I stare, awestruck, while Tall-Boy sputters. Shaking my head always felt like drawing too much attention, let alone cursing and splashing. I dread the glint in others' eyes, how I'll turn from *human* to *thing* in the flick of an internal switch the moment they realize I'm different. Vocal training hasn't come as easily to me as other girls still recovering from early testosterone infection. Some self-teach or find others to teach them. A few like their voices and insist everyone else had better deal with it.

I should be grateful that silence is my friend, that others don't clock me at a glance and figure out how I'm different from other girls. Lucky little Laurie started estro at fourteen.

Most days, I keep strict posture and bite my tongue. I would never throw soda into anyone's face. Had Tall-Boy challenged me instead of Allison, I would have agreed to whatever game he wanted. Boys like him twist sorcery on their tongues. They insist you play with them, and I'm easily witched.

Allison is my heroine for a few brief moments. She turns to stride from the table, a victorious warrior abandoning a corpse-choked battlefield. Carbonized droplets skitter down Tall-Boy's face while his friends laugh at him.

But then he weaves sorcery. "Chill, sweetie," he says, wiping a paper napkin down his face.

She turns to snap at him, dark hair coiling: "Chill yourself, asshole. Goodbye."

He leans over the table, and I see the witchcraft swirl in his piercing eyes. "Somebody has an attitude problem," he says. "It was just a joke."

Allison's lip curls back, but she hesitates. Her gaze darts back and forth, uncertain, sizing up witnesses and how they might judge her reaction. Was she the kind of girl who couldn't take a joke? She had to get her words just right or else see the dining hall condemn her as a stuck-up killjoy for all time.

"Try—" she starts, fighting tooth and nail to get the words out. "Try. Being. Funny."

Tall-Boy turns on his *debate me* voice. "Humor's subjective," he said, smooth and smarmy. "Asking me to adjust for you when we barely know each other, that's completely irrational." His eyes stab through her, reading when she'll try to speak again. He doesn't let her. "Just a joke," he repeats, this time coated in slime.

Allison's lips fight her face to make words. I don't know what she would say if she could speak. I would like to.

Instead, the silence clamps over Allison's paling complexion, her dark hair shimmering with milky starlight. She clutches her gut, as if the unspoken words now burn her belly. Her legs stagger back from the table.

Tall-Boy and his friends lean in, like they know what's about to happen. Sorcerers must have that power.

Allison's skin ripples. Every muscle twitches. If there's a sound building toward what's about to happen, I can't hear it beneath the dining hall din, Allison rendered silent. I read words in her face, the ones that have done this. Just a joke. Attitude problem. Irrational.

And then she has no face. Her body flashes out, a sudden supernova of white light and viscera. I cover my eyes, but the boys keep looking, their heat oozing over the table, dwarfing Allison's cold, starlit explosion.

She doesn't even scream.

When I finally uncover my eyes, there's nothing left of Allison. The white-light explosion has burned away her every cell. She's erased, the boys having silenced her forever.

I'm not the only one looking—the place where she stood has the entire dining hall's attention except for Tall-Boy and his friends. They're looking around, making sure this explosion has been seen and understood.

They meant to make an example of her, and they have.

They leave us then, point made. We freshman girls sit quiet, out of respect for our deceased hallmate. The moment of silence stretches to dinner's end. Back in the dorms, someone is sobbing.

Not me. I've seen quiet horror. In high school, boys used to silence with fists and boots; here they use words. This is the way of college.

Have my hallmates absorbed the lesson?

Quiet girls don't get clocked. We aren't made examples.

Quiet girls don't explode.

EMOTIONAL

I watch the chattier freshman girls when crossing the quad or getting coffee at the open-air campus center—the ones who haven't learned.

One of Tall-Boy's friends reminds me that silence is a blessing. He circles the chatty girls, a shark sizing up swimmers, and intrudes with his *debate me* voice, egging the girls to engage him on human rights or politics or some superhero movie. Given time, one will speak, and then he mocks, and interrupts, and chastises. He puts her in her place. When she's upset, he calls her "emotional," and it's a silencing nail hammered through her tongue. She's learning terror, one syllable at a time.

Unspoken words can't escape. I watch her swallow them, and they stew in her guts like trapped gas in a mine. The more she tries to talk, the worse the pressure. It's slow for some girls, quick for others. Sometimes, when crossing campus, I hear a distant eruption, and I know we've lost another.

Survival requires silence. This is the way of college.

When do the boys turn from freshmen to sorcerers?

Who teaches them the silence spell-words?

Why don't they warn us before it's too late?

Allison wouldn't have come here had she known what Tall-Boy's tongue would do to her. She wasn't the type to be silent.

Except getting a rise from her was Tall-Boy's game. She didn't know better—how could any of us? Freshmen mouths might spit fire, but we know nothing of spell-words.

Our fingers are smarter. On the way out of the dining hall one evening, I steal a knife.

IRRATIONAL

Alone in the dormitory shower, I slide the knife down my upper arm and cut a small letter into my skin—A. The shape is ragged; the blade could be sharper. I tell myself that this is how I'll remember Allison when we took no selfies together; there is no body, no candlelight vigil.

We're afraid our gathering at campus center will lure the boys. They would hear our sneakers squeaking across cobblestone and be drawn like sharks to blood in the water.

I want the second letter to be L, and then L-I-S-O-N, but I'm no longer certain Allison had two L's. Instead of overthinking it, I let the blade take over.

Knives have always made sense to me. Hormone therapy has

treated my features down to a cellular level, but deeper than that, our flesh holds bad habits holy. I thought I quit cutting myself in middle school, but a smoker smokes when the chips are down, and a cutter cuts. Transition during high school only pressed the pause button.

Still, I haven't been trapped in that *what am I?* body for years. Things have changed, even the cutting.

When I glance at the knife's work, I find the A is not the beginning, but the center. Before it, I've carved J-U-S-T. After, I've carved a J. I finish what the knife began and carve O-K-E myself.

I carve further spell-words. It's nothing like my old cutting: every bleeding stroke less about dulling psychological pain, and more about creating protective sigils. Silence spells will find themselves carved in my skin and scurry back to their masters. The boys can't witch me with words I've bled.

That's the theory, anyway.

SMILE

There's a trick to keeping boys from telling you to smile. Most girls ignore or retort, but "smile" here is another silence spell. No comebacks, only combustion.

The trick is to always smile. The worst these boys can say is "Smile bigger" or "Show some teeth," but they never do. No matter how rancid I feel inside, my cheeks tug the corners of my lips. The expression is reflex now; no need to think, no effort needed.

I probably smile in my sleep.

Maybe it's that façade of cheery disposition that draws this boy to me as I cross campus center. He has a wolfish face, jaw hugged by scruffy dark hair, but his eyes look wide and unassuming, almost innocent. Their pretty gaze doesn't fit his lupine form, two damp orbs stolen from some gentle giant.

His voice is likewise sweet. "This sounds weird, and it's okay if you don't want to talk to me, but I just—sorry, I'm not good at this. Hello."

When I wave at him, he smiles, and my lips tug a little tighter from my teeth.

"You got a name?" he asks.

An invitation to speak, not like Tall-Boy's prodding. I tell Wolf-Boy my name, keeping my tone neutral, and I never stop smiling no matter the syllables. Keeping my voice tender to temper his. Sweet as he might seem, he's still a boy at Sutton University. I cannot trust him.

He's flummoxed though, makes sure to say my name as many times as can fit in his sentences, like it might flit away if he doesn't catch it. He chats at me until we reach the edge of the dorms, when a growl cuts through my body.

I slide a concerned hand over my middle. Does this count as breaking my silence? Will Wolf-Boy cast a spell?

"That's adorable." One arm folds around my elbow, and he leads me from the dorms. "Let's grab dinner. My stomach's rumbling too."

I let him escort me toward the dining hall, my face smiling to mirror his, but I scowl inside. That growl wasn't my churning stomach.

It felt like my skin.

CALM DOWN

Outside the dining hall entrance, I excuse myself to the ladies' room. Wolf-Boy doesn't roll his eyes or chastise. Maybe the bar is too low at Sutton University, in this world, but his lack of impatience feels like hope.

I slip into a stall and pull up my shirt. I've carved letters beneath the short side of my ribcage, as if I-R-R-A-T-I-O-N-A-L can pretend that hormone treatment grows the absent strip of bone. Around the letters, skin ripples, a pond disturbed by thrashing fish.

Like Allison's skin before the end.

Maybe college just does this to girls, tells our skin to run away, fast as it can.

Or has carving the spell-word into my flesh stuck the sorcery inside? The words manifest, but unlike for other girls, my skin's set to unravel, muscle sloughing from bone. Different girls might self-destruct in different kinds of ways.

Not an explosion, but a meltdown. How long until the sorcery kills me?

If I'm dying, I don't want to die alone, and since there's no one else in the ladies' room, I find Wolf-Boy in the dining hall. I'm not sure if he's genuinely interested in me or if he's playing games like Tall-Boy. If I step away, tell Wolf-Boy, "Goodbye," will he toss a spell-word or let me go?

Worse, if I like him, will he want me to speak more? Boys can be harsh. Sometimes I envy the girls who like other girls. I used to radiate the sun, but hormones cooled my blood. The only girl I ever dated had hands and feet as cold as mine, lizards attached to our limbs. Boys are furnaces, and I crave the warmth.

Sometimes attraction is that simple.

We eat slowly, and I let him do the talking. Never spell-words, always gentle. He urges a few words from me here and there, but they're scaffolding through which he builds his side of the conversation.

"Where are you from?" he asks.

"West," I say, tender yet neutral, still smiling while I chew.

He asks, "What's your major?"

"English."

He has opinions there, my answer prompting his every thought on Literature classes, majors, and degrees. On the surface, I hear his critique. Deeper, I wonder if an onslaught of opinion is another means to silence me, a complex string of pieces that form a spell. Should I be terrified? My skin growls, but the dining hall din smothers the sound.

Even my body is silenced, but that's better than exploding.

When will the meltdown take me? Do Wolf-Boy and I have time for kissing and touching first? He's barely an acquaintance, but if I lead him to my dorm room, he'll follow. Will a nod be my consent for more? He'll have to notice the spell-words carved into my skin. I might even drag him into the meltdown. And shouldn't I mention how I'm different from other girls? My last boyfriend knew before he asked me out. Will Wolf-Boy still see that I'm human, or will I become a thing?

When it comes to girls, sometimes boys see little difference. Even the ones with sweet eyes.

As we leave the dining hall, his arm once again hooked around mine, I realize we're not going to find out how he sees me. Campus is no place for closeness or honesty. Another freshman girl cowers at the edge of the dorms, caught in Tall-Boy's shadow. His friends linger close. Girls keep their distance, weaving around the scene or watching from doorways.

Wolf-Boy strides toward the cluster, a solitary angel who might make a difference in this undergrad hell. A familiar itch crosses my skin, the kind when you want to drag a boy by his jacket into your bedroom and then tear away that jacket and everything else.

The nameless freshman girl turns to speak to him, probably to plead. Her face is scrunched, desperate.

Wolf-Boy holds up an open palm. "Calm down," he says. "What's the trouble?"

Desire's itch washes off my skin, and the growling ripple returns. Tall-Boy and his friends lean in, expectant, but Wolf-Boy stares oblivious. My sweet wolf has no idea he's spoken another silencing spell.

I can't watch. Without waiting for him, I skirt around the crowd and run for my dorm's front doors. He doesn't mean to cast spells, but he can't help it. They are the words he knows. How long until he slings them my way? I catch the girl, out of the corner of my eye, wrapping her arms around her torso as if trying to hold herself together. She's already reached her limit from Tall-Boy. Wolf-Boy's pressure is too much. She's done.

As I rush inside my dorm hall, I hear her explode.

NEUROTIC

My skin twitches harder each day. Wolf-Boy watched me run, and now he haunts my dorm hall. "Laurie, you there?" he calls, but I never answer. He might tell me to calm down, and I won't risk it.

No one guides him to my door. We girls are frightened, and the boys down the hall don't know my name. Those immune won't answer him—the musician who speaks more Mandarin than English, the history major with hearing aids, the non-binary students scattered between binary hall designations. They can't share their safety.

Not that I blame them; I can't share my knife.

And I can't quit cutting. My skin growls non-stop, every pore a mouth caught mid-snarl. Beneath the shower's spattering rain, I try to relieve word-driven pressure, but whispers aren't enough. Something inside me wants to roar.

Only carving settles my skin. I imagine spell-words Wolf-Boy might lace onto his opinions were we to peel each other's clothes off and bare my cutting. R-I-D-I-C-U-L-O-U-S. N-E-U-R-O-T-I-C. T-O-O and then M-U-C-H. I empathize with tattoo lovers—I'm running out of spare skin.

Still, no meat sloughs off. If I've averted the meltdown, will I still explode? Too many theories swirl inside—maybe I'm too different from the other girls. Maybe surviving attempted self-destruction years ago has helped build antibodies. Maybe the carvings do their job so that Tall-Boy and friends can't destroy me. Maybe I haven't given them a reason.

And Wolf-Boy? In a darkened room, he might not notice my carvings. He might not care how I'm different. If my fingertips coax him to growl like a wolf, he might not hear my skin do the same.

But Wolf-Boy, Tall-Boy—they're of one nature. The boys pronounce themselves individuals for conflicting views on ethics, culture, and history, but they're each sharks in the same ocean. Tall-Boy the Cruel, but he's just joking. Wolf-Boy the Cruel, but *calm down* because he doesn't mean it. Surely the others have spiced up their cruelty to help live with themselves.

Excuses, excuses.

Our upperclassmen know when to be silent and when to speak—when spoken to. Those of us who survive our freshman year will grow into sophomores if we learn the same, a mandatory class we obliviously enrolled in upon orientation. Sutton University's spell-word crucible will destroy the rest.

In the end, we girls will likewise be of one nature. I won't be a different kind of girl anymore. Isn't that the dream?

As my skin ripples, filled with wolves and leopards and every growling angry beast that's ever walked this world, I wonder—if that's the dream then what's the nightmare?

And the boys? What's *their* nightmare?

ATTITUDE PROBLEM

Weeks have passed since Allison's death, but I finally muster a candlelight vigil for her. For all the girls who've exploded. I pass notes through the freshman dorm, meant for the girls, but others will find them, too. They'll spread the word.

The lure.

We gather after sunset at campus center to raise candles. This moment of silence might have stretched until midnight, but I hear Tall-Boy's snide voice at the crowd's edge. He's playing the shark, testing us for weaknesses. Sizing up who to bite.

I don't understand why he does it. Probing the freshman population for what he considers girlfriend material? A lackluster comedian hunting an audience for when he's *just joking*? Does he like to watch us brim with starlight and suffer explosions?

Or does he do it because he can?

I muscle through the vigil's crowd and find he's not alone. His cluster of friends traipse behind him in matching button-downs, eyes on their leader. I storm between him and the other girls, my candlestick spattering on cobblestone. Skin and mouth growl together as I hurl insults, telling him exactly what I think of Tall-Boy's unjust jokes, creepy grin, and shark-like face.

He smirks at first, but his confident mask crumbles when his friends snicker. Spell-words spit off his lips, sprinkle my face.

I shout an onslaught of opinions to rival Wolf-Boy's. Every word's emotional, my voice clumsy, my skin snarling, and I'm not sorry for it, and I can't stop. I won't stop. That's why Tall-Boy, tongue flustered, finally storms forward and shoves my shoulders.

I crash onto the cobblestones. My skin quits growling, the pain welcome, and I can't help the cracking shout that shoots up my throat. It is an old voice I keep meaning to leave behind.

The glint shifts in Tall-Boy's eyes. "Oh," he says, piercing gaze at last seeing me. Clocking me. His barracuda smile returns.

The moment stretches in pregnant silence. I've turned from *human* to *thing* in his eyes, but I don't mind because that's how he sees every girl here. It's validating in a terrible way. He wants to sling spell-words fashioned solely for me, the kinds of slurs you'll find for a dime a dozen on any street.

But I don't let him finish. I barely let him start.

"That's why it doesn't work," he says. "Because you're not really a—"

I stand quick and thrust my face into his. "I'm not done," I snap.

His tongue limpens, and his jaw goes slack. No slurs, no spells. No jokes. The words slide down his esophagus and into his stomach, where they froth and rumble.

He tries again. "You—"

I lean closer. "Don't interrupt me."

Again, he swallows his words. His friends aren't snickering now; they realize in fits and starts what's happening to their tall leader. Behind me, the girls cluster. They're still silent, but they're watching.

Someone who isn't silent appears from the gloom beyond the crowd—Wolf-Boy. His scruffy face doesn't smile now. He scowls at Tall-Boy, who's gripping his guts, and then at me. Wolf-Boy thinks he understands, but he's thought that before and been wrong.

Still, he tries. "No need to fight, right?" he asks.

Each word rings earnest. I know he only means the best, can't see the damage he does, how he props up boys like Tall-Boy and shatters girls like the nameless freshman he told to calm down. It would be easy to fall into his oblivious arms and let his furnace warm me.

But I can't.

His mouth opens again to ask, "Why don't we just calm—"

"No," I snap.

Like a scolded dog, he bows his head, and I imagine his ears drooping. I won't let him tell me to calm, or settle, or chill. Not anyone else, either. Good intentions don't matter; a spell-word is a spell-word. Wolf-Boy has his innocent mistakes, Tall-Boy has his humor and viciousness.

And we girls have our vengeance.

I sling spell-words at Tall-Boy. Ones he knows, like *irrational* and *attitude problem*. Ones he doesn't, like *no*. I speak ones specially for him, like *sad* and *worthless* and *empty*. The harder he tries to smirk through it, the deeper my tongue carves them into his body.

Other freshman girls chime in. They only speak the words I use, but an echo is better than silence. We know what this will do to him now, and we mean it. We aren't joking. We are far from calm.

Because girls can be cruel, too.

And I make sure everyone sees. Tall-Boy will turn example at the center of campus. This is the way of college. Sutton University might trigger spell-words to explosions, but we've all been silenced before. Tall-Boy hasn't. He's never been put in his place, has no tolerance to the pressure. It builds quickly inside him.

I strip off my jacket, roll up my sleeves and leggings, expose my midriff and ribs and every spell-word etched into my skin. A new carving tattoos my sternum, and I speak it now. It echoes the first exploding girl. One last spell-word to bring white light bursting from the first exploding boy.

Silently, I thank Allison for teaching it to me.

GOODBYE

ARTOWN CORRECTIONAL CENTER

Patty Templeton

Over the Years. Central Illinois.

Lefty was friends with a slug named Gary. Then Lefty was gone.

The sun knew Smith as Darnell because Smith introduced himself during his first stroll in the Yard. He said, "Hey, sun. I'm Darnell. I missed you." Because a person's gotta joke to somebody. Then Darnell was gone.

Williams wasn't the best. Wasn't the worst. Then he was gone.

The prison librarian noticed when Tamarna stopped coming in for sci-fi, Howell no longer requested workout guides, and Blackson hadn't been in for magazines, but the prison librarian was busier than deathbed regret and never asked where they'd gone.

Duke was a fuckface motherfucker and no one gave a hooting shit when they realized he was gone.

Every third letter Hakim's sister, Rosette, wrote him, Hakim would answer. Tell the girl to quit being boy-crazy and keep getting As in biology. It'd been nine letters and Rosette hadn't heard from Hakim. He was gone.

People got gone every week. Someone always noticed, but if people thought *you* don't matter, what *you notice* didn't matter either. Take Rosette. That girl did everything from bus five hours to Artown Correctional Center to try and visit her big brother, to a solo sit-in at the governor's office when ACC "couldn't find him." Didn't matter. Politicians don't listen to Black girls; they move them along.

Gone is vague. Gone makes it sound like caged people poofed out of existence. Which they did, but then they (usually) showed up.

Discovered dead before most staff knew they were missing. *Inmate-on-inmate violence* was the warden's report. Didn't matter that they were sometimes off-property. One guy was in a forest three miles away. That got on the news. He'd been gone so long his face had flattened, but then *Top Gun* became the highest-grossing film of 1986, making $177 million in America alone, so everyone stopped talking about it. Him.

People inside didn't know how folks got gone, but they knew they weren't killing each other. Nobody outside listened. Folks inside went quiet, hoped if you didn't notice the monster, the monster wouldn't notice you.

Which, unfortunately, ain't true.

1993.

Mr. Miller had been a Supply Administrator at Artown Correctional Center for twenty-two years. He liked making lists. He liked checking lists. He liked to think he created good by ordering goods. ACC was a mid-sized prison and Mr. Miller solely staffed Supply Administration. He never understood why people fussed about solitary confinement. Solitude suited him fine.

Supply Admin was innocuously named but important sounding. It never faced cutbacks and Mr. Miller was rarely invited to leadership meetings. No one questioned his role at ACC because no one much noticed him, except the three correctional officers who buzzed him through entry points to his office.

Mr. Miller had a different yellow tie for each weekday. They brightened his windowless office at the end of a remote storage corridor on the first floor. Tight space but uncluttered. His desk was in the center and faced a gray door with a wire glass window. Shelves on one wall, filing cabinets on the other. Above him, the infirmary. He spent his days between an unused stairwell and an unstaffed dead records office. Mr. Miller only left his office to inventory closets, collect supply request sheets from the tray in the employee lounge, and to acquire human stock.

Mr. Miller's predecessor, Mr. Jones, said the Thing only ate Black stock. Mr. Miller had supplied it white stock in a time crunch back in

'79, and nothing terrible happened. Nevertheless, according to the feed ledger—a thin, tall, yellow book that had 122 years of recorded meals by Mr. Spenser (from 1871-1921) and Mr. Jones (from 1921-1971) and now by Mr. Miller (from 1971-present) —the Thing had only been fed the one white guy. It wasn't in good taste to break tradition. Or lucky. Since then, Mr. Miller endeavored to strictly follow Mr. Jones' directions. He supposed it was unfair, but he didn't make the rules. There was probably a scientific reason for what the Thing ate, and it was much better to feed the Thing than be fed to it. Besides, it's not like Mr. Miller was racist. He liked *The Cosby Show*.

Hermando Gil liked mopping. Got him outta his cell. Almost felt normal, especially near first floor admin where there was drywall and linoleum instead of stone and steel. An old-timer'd told him they made ACC back in the 1850s. Admin though? Had a re-do in the '40s. Cramped halls. Fluorescent lights. Like high school minus lockers.

Hermando was a trustee, which meant he had a blue jumpsuit instead of orange and ACC trusted him to do operational grunt work. He did janitorial maintenance Monday through Friday. He had a month left and wasn't a flight risk. Hermando did good work. Kept shit off his record. No C.O. hounded him too much. Mostly. Cops are cops even when they're guards.

Mopping would've been better if he got paid more than fourteen cents an hour. Took three hours to buy a snack-size Cheetos. But movement was good and he thought about Hermando's Cave. He was gonna open a comic book shop. Gonna have a purple couch and a pile of ratty comics that kids could read after school, with the expensive stuff behind the counter outta reach of the little shitheads. Probably sell candy bars—the good stuff. Butterfingers and Twix. A room in the back where he'd do D&D. Have a pink neon sign. A hottie'd come in wearing spandex bike shorts and a *Sandman* shirt wanting to talk about *Tales from the Crypt* and she'd slip him her number after she bought—

"You," Mr. Miller called from down the hall.

Hermando looked at Mr. Miller in his doorway. "Yes, sir?"

"I need you to reach something."

"I'm not supposed to," Hermando started. He rubbed a scarred ear. His ma had turned from the stove with a pan and he'd been little and in the way.

"Should I call your C.O.? It's that thick one, right? Pierce? Think he'll like coming down to watch me watch you get a file from a drawer?"

"No, sir. I'm coming, sir." Hermando left the mop in the bucket.

"I have back troubles," Mr. Miller said. "That drawer sticks. Open it." He pointed to the prettiest filing cabinet Hermando'd ever seen. Looked like Sherlock Holmes shit. Oak and tall. Brass handles and matching label holders. Drawers stacked in twos on top of one oversized drawer at its base. Maybe he'd get one for the shop.

Mr. Miller shut the office door.

During two weeks of training in 1971, Mr. Miller saw inside the oversized drawer. It didn't open to files. It opened to a dirty hole in the ground. Hair tangled in root clumps. Teeth mashed into clay.

Mr. Jones was very specific. Mr. Miller was to feed the Thing every Friday at five in the evening. He was never to personally open the drawer on a Friday unless he wanted to be eaten. He was never to discuss the Thing. The higher-ups didn't know about it and if they did Mr. Jones was quite clear that they'd cock everything up and who knows what the Thing would do or how many times it would need to be fed then. "Might even come outta the damn drawer. Who you think it's gonna eat first?" Mr. Jones said, blowing cigarette smoke from Mr. Miller's future swivel chair.

Mr. Jones asked if Mr. Miller had questions, but after witnessing his first feeding, Mr. Miller didn't. It was a good job. A job Mr. Miller wanted. It had a pension. Asking questions cost time and never paid extra. Everything was straightforward. Order supplies and feed a... well, a Thing.

· · ·

It was Nurse Beatrix Rosette Shelda's three-month anniversary at Artown Correctional Center. She didn't like it. Razor wire on barbed wire on limestone walls. Everything about Artown made her feel small, but she guessed that's what gothic architecture was supposed to do. Friends called her Rosette. Everyone at ACC used Nurse Shelda.

Nurse Shelda thought the movies maybe exaggerated prisons and it wouldn't be that bad—it was the '90s for godssake—but it was. Today, some senator stopped by. Not one she voted for. He wanted a picture by the "oldest cell in the Midwest." It was occupied. It was an outdoor box—four by seven. Light came in from the barred door which also let in animals and bugs and inclement weather. It seemed illegal. Head Nurse Baker assured Nurse Shelda it wasn't. The cell was from 1853 and had a steel bunk bed; it figured some senator wanted a picture being "tough on crime" in front of it.

She shouldn't be smoking. Nurse Shelda told herself she'd quit for real. Even so, she lit a cig as soon as she buzzed out of Artown. She had a three-minute walk across the parking lot. She refused to smoke in her car.

It was Friday. She wanted a frozen Alfredo dinner with a glass of pinot noir and an episode of *Designing Women*. She liked to think she was a Julia Sugarbaker, but she was closer to a Mary Jo. No elegant business lady but definitely a sarcastic single mother of two.

The twins had a sleepover at her mom's. Nurse Shelda needed a night off. She wasn't squeamish. She'd worked critical care at Artown Hospital. She'd seen what drunks with M-80s were capable of and how a motorcycle kickstand could impale someone after a wheelie went wrong. She took the job at ACC because she thought it'd be more check-ups and less gore, which it was. Sort of. But a lot of people died at Artown. At least one a week. Which was less than critical care, but most deaths at ACC didn't make sense. Head Nurse Baker said it was gang fights, but men didn't look roughed up, aside from sometimes a missing tooth or fingernail. They looked drained. Skin ashy as sick wood.

Nurse Shelda walked past her hatchback. She always gave herself to the edge of the parking lot to finish a cig.

She knew why she took the job and kept it. Rosette wanted to see inside of ACC. She wanted to see where Hakim lived and disappeared from. She was "over it." It'd been a decade. She had a therapist. But she wasn't over it-over it. She knew she wasn't going to Columbo around Artown to find out what happened to Hakim. Her brother was gone and staying gone. But she also thought Hakim was a good kid who'd done a stupid thing. Not even that stupid. Caught with weed and then he was in jail and then he was gone. But she could see where things ended. Tell her mom about it.

There was a body.

She blinked. Shook her head. There was a dead man face-down in a blue trustee jumpsuit where the asphalt met grass. He was for-sure dead because she'd flicked her cigarette before noticing and it'd landed on the back of his shaved head. Nurse Shelda brushed the cigarette off, noticed the scar on his ear, and ran back to ACC for help.

Before the Thing ate him, Hermando Gil had signed the ledger.

Mr. Miller had feedstock sign the ledger because Mr. Jones had feedstock sign the ledger because Mr. Spenser had feedstock sign the ledger. Mr. Spenser began the ledger in October of 1871. He, too, liked making lists. He liked checking lists. He liked to think he created good by recording goods.

"No one can withdraw files without signing, even if you're withdrawing files to immediately hand to me," Mr. Miller explained to Hermando.

The ledger was atop the filing cabinet. The date and time were already filled in. Hermando signed his name, wrote his ID number, and opened the drawer.

An immediate lurch. Then crunching.

None of the Thing's keepers looked at it head-on. It was too big to comfortably consider. Mr. Spenser told Mr. Jones to observe the Thing out of the side of his eye, so that's what Mr. Jones did and that's what Mr. Jones told Mr. Miller to do. It was unsettling for Mr. Miller even to see it from side-eye so he stopped looking altogether. Mr. Miller flipped through *Reader's Digest* until the slush-chew quieted. Then he carefully nudged the drawer shut with a brown loafer, put the magazine in his desk, closed the ledger, and left.

He didn't slow his blue Buick LeSabre to see what the commotion was on the other side of the lot. He could still make happy hour at Bennigan's.

Two people saw Hermando Gil before Nurse Shelda did, but neither spoke up.

C.O. Pierce supervised two trustees scrubbing showers. A showerhead rattled. Then another. And another. The drain under Pierce's boot rattled. He moved his foot. An amber eye watched him. Pierce blinked. Only suds. He yelled at the trustees to get back to work.

Smokes folded clothes in the laundry. He was alone. Until he wasn't. Something crunched behind him. Crunched again. The only thing that was supposed to be behind Smokes was a line of dryers and a concrete block wall. Smokes climbed a dryer and looked through a high, greasy window into the boiler room. Dark. Pipes. Steam rose past a red light. A brown arm emerged from the steam. Got yanked back. Smokes fell off the dryer. Almost busted his ass. Didn't climb back up because he didn't want any part of whatever that was.

The Next Friday.

"Don't you think it's strange?" Nurse Shelda said.

The employee lounge was deserted.

Head Nurse Baker filled their coffee mugs. "It's scary. An inmate escaped. How did that even happen?"

"That's what I'm saying. How could he get to the parking lot?"

"I'm glad he was dead. He could've stolen your car. Or kidnapped you. I can't even think about it."

"Why would a trustee run with less than a month left?"

"Who knows? If I worried on every odd thing, I wouldn't still be here."

"What odd things?"

Head Nurse Baker looked at the vending machines. There was the rancid fishstick smell that overtook the stairwell by the dead records office. And the chuffing noise in the vent in corridor B. And three years ago, she was in the toilet, heard a thump, and opened the stall to find a dead man under the sink. "Doesn't matter. Keep your head down, clock in, and clock out," Head Nurse Baker said. "And speaking of, here's Dr. Jagge's list of staff avoiding flu shots. All in admin. Get 'em."

"Always admin," Nurse Shelda said and took the list.

The rest of the day, Rosette worked her way through Dr. Jagge's list. Last up: Maxwell Miller in Supply Admin. She asked two different C.O.s for directions, and it ended up being directly below the infirmary in a hall everyone seemed to forget existed. It was nearly shift change. All she wanted was to get in and out.

She almost knocked. But didn't.

She didn't scream either. Had no breath. She backed away from the door. Shoulders turned stone. No one else in the hall. She looked at her medical bag. Then at the door. She couldn't have seen what she thought she saw. Nurse Shelda rolled her shoulders, cursed fatigue, and walked back.

She did see what she saw.

A trustee's blue legs were perpendicular to the floor. Thrashing, kicking, and disappearing into the bottom drawer of a filing cabinet. A man with a yellow tie sat behind a desk with a magazine.

It was absurd. So absurd that, for the second time, Rosette couldn't believe she'd seen it. In real life, people didn't get sucked into drawers. She knocked. The hall's fluorescent lights buzzed.

Mr. Miller opened the door.

"What can I do for you?"

"Mandatory flu shot," Nurse Shelda said and stepped past him into the office.

"I don't need one," Mr. Miller said.

"Dr. Jagge's orders," she said, putting her bag on the man's desk.

She looked behind it. There was a fancy filing cabinet in the corner. Drawer closed. Clean floor.

Mr. Miller rolled his sleeve and watched her.

She disinfected her hands and put on gloves. She had the terrible impulse to make small talk.

"Was the tuna good?" she asked, uncapping the needle.

"What?"

The office was clean, but there was an odor. Like tuna microwaved too long. And mud.

"What did you have for lunch?" She pinched his upper arm skin and jabbed the needle in at a forty-five degree angle.

"I missed lunch."

"Sorry to hear that." She swabbed his arm, taped cotton to it, and noticed a scuff on the wall near the filing cabinet. It had happened. Someone had kicked the wall.

Mr. Miller looked over his shoulder to see what she stared at. "What's your name?"

"Shelda. Started three months ago." She packed her med bag. Who had gone in the filing cabinet? Why would he put someone in the filing cabinet? Were they dead?

"Welcome to Artown, Nurse Shelda."

"You, too!" she mumbled. "I mean, happy Friday!"

She walked out.

Mr. Miller sniffed the air and then his armpit. Didn't smell anything. He took a baby wipe from a desk drawer to clean the wall scuff.

Rosette made it to the infirmary, through security, and then to her hatchback before shaking. She didn't know what to do or who to tell. What could she say? "Mr. Miller let his drawer eat someone"? Who would believe that? Where's the proof? The Warden already didn't like her.

What could she say?

What could she say?

· · ·

After his first Friday as head of ACC, Warden Kowalski told his wife at dinner, "It sounds like a rhinoceros eating a watermelon directly under my desk." Which was a pity because it was an otherwise pleasurable teak and burl desk.

"How strange, darling," Mrs. Kowalski said and served him potatoes.

The next Friday, Warden Kowalski said, "It happened again."

"What did, darling?" Mrs. Kowalski asked and served him meatloaf.

"That ugly sound. Nearly turned my stomach."

"When does it occur?" she asked and served him peas.

"5 p.m. Right before I leave."

"Why don't you start five minutes earlier and leave five minutes earlier on Fridays? Then you won't hear it." She passed him the ketchup.

He smiled. He had the smartest, best wife, even if her meatloaf was dry.

Thirty-nine years later, Warden Kowalski still left at 4:55 p.m. on Fridays.

It wasn't hard for Nurse Shelda to pick up the next day's shift. Nobody liked working Saturdays. What was tricky was convincing security staff she brought a Panasonic Palmcorder into ACC to track unusual flu symptoms. What was ethically dubious was passing a trustee named Smokes a carton of cigarettes to make some noise. And, really, she thought it'd be more difficult to convince the C.O. to let her into Supply Administration, but he couldn't care less about her excuse of forgetting vaccine vials there yesterday.

C.O. Pierce unlocked the door and flicked on the light. He sniffed, pulled a face, but didn't say anything.

Rosette scanned the room. The wall was clean.

"Need help?" he asked.

Before Nurse Shelda could answer, there was a crash and a violent holler down the hall.

Pierce said, "I'm shutting this. You're safe." He jogged from the room. The door locked shut.

She had five minutes max. Rosette took out the camcorder. Turned it on. She panned around the room and zoomed in on Mr. Miller's desk. Flat calendar. Pen cup. Three black binders. Typewriter. Brass name plate. Inside the top drawer: Tums, pencils, *Reader's Digest*. Another drawer: legal pads. Last drawer: baby wipes, oatmeal, bowl, spoon, hotplate. She moved to the filing cabinet.

Old, important-looking book up there. She stuffed it in her med bag.

She recorded the drawers. The top two were labeled "Spenser." The next, "Jones." The next. "Miller." She grabbed the first inch of files from each name and stuffed them in the med bag, too.

The bottom drawer wasn't labeled. She opened it.

There was a hole. A reeking hole.

The odor reminded her of a patient who couldn't stop crapping after eating a bacteria-laden clam chowder. Nurse Shelda dry heaved, wretch-wobbled…and dropped the camcorder. It fell into the hole.

Someone yelled down the hall.

Nurse Shelda swallowed her breakfast back down. The camcorder wasn't hers. She'd borrowed it from her mom's boyfriend. It cost more than she made in a week. She shoved her hands and head into the drawer. Saw the camera. Was snagged on something. Reached. Scooted forward. Reached. The hole could fit her on her hands and knees, but she didn't have time to crawl further in.

The hole vibrated. A centipede dropped in front of her face. Her hand slammed on something sharp. She scrambled away from the hole, landed on her rear, and kicked the drawer shut.

A human fingernail was lodged in Nurse Shelda's left palm. Jagged. Gray. She pulled it out. Went to her bulging med bag. Swabbed the wound. Taped cotton to it.

The door clicked open.

"Find it?" C.O. Pierce asked.

"Huh?" Nurse Shelda said, smoothing her hair.

"The medicine?"

"Oh, mhmm." She tapped her bag. "What happened out there?"

"Trustee fell. Yelled his head off. Said a ghost pushed him.

Probably only a sprained ankle and drugs. Had to drag him to psych. Goddamn idiot."

An old book, a stack of files, and the camcorder gone.

Rosette couldn't bring herself to look at the ledger when she got home from what ended up being a busy shift. She tried after the twins were asleep but cried so hard she puked. She couldn't stop wondering whose fingernail had pierced her palm.

Another New Week.

Rosette almost told her mom she thought Mr. Miller was a serial killer, but it was a horrible lot of worry to give, let alone at Sunday supper. And if her mother knew, she would tell old-head Harvey about his lost camcorder.

Monday, after the twins went to school, Rosette sat at her kitchen table with coffee and the evidence. She sorted the files full of receipts and random junk until a minute to a migraine. No idea.

The book though, it was a list of people.

The first name: Abraham Brown, ID number 119. He signed his name with an X, which was witnessed by Samuel Spenser at 5 p.m. on Friday, October 13, 1871. The last name: Arlo Q. Tahmet. Between them, over a hundred years of signatures. It was too much to read, but she recognized the second-to-last name. Hermando Gil. Signed the day she found him in the parking lot.

Reading the book made her guts cramp and quake.

On Monday, Mr. Miller knew someone had been in his office. His oatmeal drawer was slightly open. He didn't leave drawers slightly open. It bothered him, but nothing was stolen so he didn't lodge a complaint. Besides, Mondays were busy. There were shipments to inventory and data sheets to input.

If the weekend's supply request sheets hadn't been so heaping, Mr. Miller would have noticed his ledger was missing.

Head Nurse Baker didn't say good morning to Nurse Shelda on Tuesday. Instead, she asked, "Did you hear?"

"What?" Nurse Shelda said.

"Another one."

"Another what?"

"Escapee!" Head Nurse Baker squeaked.

"Where?"

Head Nurse Baker stacked latex glove boxes. "Under a pick-up by the guard tower on Sunday."

"Who was it?"

"Arlo something or other. Didn't see his chart. DOA."

Mr. Miller's Tuesday tie didn't cheer him up. He couldn't pinpoint what, but something was wrong. He thought maybe he was catching a bug, but he felt fine.

He did what calmed him. He dusted the doorframe. Then the floorboards. Then his desk. Every shelf. Each filing cabinet. The ledger. Where was the ledger? Would the feeding work without the ledger? What happened if feedstock didn't sign? What happened to him? Unprecedented. Mr. Miller sat in his swivel chair and pressed fists into his eyes.

So late on Tuesday that it was actually early Wednesday, Rosette saw her brother's name.

Hakim Shelda, ID number 484842. Signed in a hand she knew. Witnessed by Maxwell Miller at 5 p.m. on Friday, March 11, 1983.

She put her fingers to the ink. Closed the book. Brought a pillow to the bathroom and cried into it where she wouldn't wake her twins.

. . .

People didn't like talking to Mr. Miller as much as he didn't like talking to them. He spent all of Wednesday and the better half of Thursday trying to find out from C.O.s. who had been in his office. That fathead Pierce finally told him it was Nurse Shelda.

She touched his drawer.

She took his ledger.

Miller dialed the infirmary.

Rosette picked up on the second ring.

"Infirmary, Nurse Shelda speaking, how can I help you?"

"Give me my ledger," Miller said.

Nurse Shelda hung up, hot. She wasn't sure if she was scared or angry. Both. She took two steps away. It rang again.

"Bring me my ledger and I won't tell Head Nurse Baker you're a thief," Miller said.

"You kill people," she said. "You ain't telling anyone a damn thing."

"I – what?"

"In your office," Nurse Shelda whisper-hissed. "My *brother* was in your office."

"I've never killed anyone," Miller said.

"I know about your fucking drawer."

Miller hung up, hot. He wasn't sure if he was scared or angry. Both. What did this woman know about his drawer? And who was her brother? Did that mean she knew about the Thing? Nobody was supposed to know about the ledger or the drawer or the Thing. Yet, she did. He didn't like the idea of feeding it a woman. It'd never been done, but she certainly couldn't keep knowing.

Nurse Shelda didn't have time to think about Miller, but she kept her eyes open for him. Her day was stacked until five with the flu, MRSA, and cancer. She almost went to Warden Kowalski's office, but, "Mr. Miller dumps people in a drawer and then they die," still sounded too stupid to say out loud. All she had were random files and a ledger that admitted tenuous connection, not crime.

It wasn't until she was driving to pick up the twins from their grandma's that Rosette thought hard about the hole. If it had a fingernail, it had other bodily materials. Evidence. But her prints were on the drawer. Her camcorder in the hole. Would that tie her to Miller's bullshit? Naw. There were a hundred years of people in that drawer and she'd only been at ACC three months. Still, she'd had cousins shoved against cars and cuffed for just breathing air. She wanted that fucker stopped, but she needed anonymity. If she could get the camcorder back, she'd have enough to send to the *Chicago Tribune*.

The Friday tie was butterscotch. It wasn't as soothing as usual. The prospect of happy hour at Bennigan's wasn't either. He felt awful. Mr. Miller wasn't used to feeling awful. He wanted his clean, quiet routine back. If that woman had kept her nose in her own paygrade none of this would have happened. She didn't trust him. He'd never done anything to anyone that mattered. He was honest. Artown functioned because of him. He got things done. But how to get *this* done? She'd never come to his office if he asked. Head Nurse Baker could make her. Or he could go to the infirmary. It would look official if he brought a clipboard. He'd wait till feeding time. He didn't want her talking at him all day. He doubted she'd have the ledger. He'd find out where she put it before she went in the drawer.

During Friday's full-on MRSA outbreak, Nurse Beatrix Rosette Shelda handled more boils, pus, and fevers than she'd seen in her life. Then there was the surface disinfecting. It was a god-awful day made worse by Miller lurking in the infirmary with a clipboard at half-past four. There wasn't an angel in heaven that could make her go near that man or his office if he was in-building. The camcorder would wait.

Mr. Miller was nervous and when he was nervous he had to pee. The infirmary had a single stall staff restroom. It was only 4:45. He had time.

. . .

Nurse Shelda saw Miller enter the bathroom.

Head Nurse Baker wheeled an elderly patient by. Nurse Shelda stopped her.

"Do you mind if I leave? Stomach's gone sour."

"All that pus probably," said Head Nurse Baker. "Take off."

"Thank you!"

"Feel better!" said the old man cuffed to the chair.

Nurse Shelda didn't hear. She was already in the stairwell.

"Where did Nurse Shelda go?" Mr. Miller asked Head Nurse Baker.

"Home," said an old man the nurse pushed in a wheelchair. He shifted a thumb to the stairwell.

Mr. Miller ran toward it.

Nurse Shelda passed Miller's office as he bounded out of the stairwell after her. She yanked on the dead records office door—locked. A closet next to it—locked. No one heard her yell for help.

Miller approached quick. She wanted to bash him over the head with his clipboard. Tried another door—unlocked—a severe violation of safety protocol. Inmates could've opened the door, gone down the steps, and congregated in the boiler room, but no one was there. Except her. Until Miller followed.

Rosette hid in a clay crawlspace that smelled like shellfish on a radiator; being in a dark hole was better than being in the wide open with a monster.

Mr. Miller looked at his Omega De Ville. 4:50.

"Nurse Shelda," he made his voice calm, "where's my ledger?"

She stayed silent. Edged further into the dark. Didn't screech when her hand dipped into what felt like cottage cheese.

Miller looked into a pipe cluster. Steam puffed. A red light flickered by a groaning machine. It was dark and he didn't like dark. It was dirty and he didn't like dirt. Hide-n-seek was beneath him.

"Nurse Shelda, we can handle this if you come out and—"

A drop of something wet and foul fell on Mr. Miller. And another. He looked up, dropped his clipboard, and screamed.

Rosette didn't want to know why Miller screamed. She turned to find out how far the hole went.

A calm man without limits was not smart. Mr. Miller fancied himself smart. He ran to the back of the boiler room.

The Thing followed.

Miller stumbled into a dark hole in the wall. He heard scrambling.

"Is that you, Shelda?"

Something sounded like a tub running-over but if someone replaced the water with Jell-O.

Rosette didn't answer. She crawled faster through tunnel-muck.

The ground vibrated.

"Go. Go now," Miller said much too close to her ass.

The noise of slick limbs traveling swiftly canceled the boiler room's clang and hiss.

"What is it?" Rosette yelled.

"The Thing!"

"What thing?" She hadn't moved this fast since ninth grade track.

Dirt clumps rained down. The hole got smaller. She ducked her head.

"Move, MOVE," said Miller.

A moist tendril curled around his ankle. He shook it off.

Rosette's head suddenly wrenched back. Her hair was caught.

"Don't stop!" Mr. Miller landed a bruising blow to her tailbone. Tried to shove her forward.

"I'm stuck."

He pushed again. Her hair was about to tear off her head.

"Stop it!"

Mr. Miller dug in for a shove.

An audible rip and shriek. Rosette left a clump of tight curls behind as her body sprawled forward. Blood trickled down her temple.

"Move!"

"I am!"

Her knuckle hit something hard. Plastic. The camcorder. She put on the wrist strap and dragged it.

The walls vibrated faster. Dirt pelted them in a steady stream.

The Thing breathed on Maxwell Miller.

"Go, go, go now!" he screamed.

Rosette slammed against the drawer and it budged open. She slammed again and rocketed out of the filing cabinet into Miller's clean, well-lighted office.

Mr. Miller felt every hair on his body. He was fine. He made it. He climbed halfway out of the drawer.

He looked up at Nurse Shelda standing in his office. Bleeding, dirty, defiant. She didn't look sorry for causing so much trouble.

She wasn't sorry.

Behind him, there was a cool wind. A wet slip. A lurch. Sharp teeth. And crunching.

Mr. Miller was yanked back into the hole.

Nurse Shelda looked into the dark until the slush-chew quieted.

He was gone.

It was gone.

Rosette backed away from the filing cabinet. She had seen the Thing. It was too big to comfortably consider, but she hadn't looked away. She hadn't screamed.

After the third Friday of not being fed, the Thing left Artown.

Three Months Later.

Chicago Tribune headline: ARTOWN CORRECTIONAL CENTER INVESTIGATED AFTER ANONYMOUS TIPSTER UNCOVERS 122 YEARS OF MURDER.

TABLEAU VIVANT

Michael Paul Gonzalez

You expect to make a living doing this?

Nella's father's voice echoed in her head. She was a living statue, something her father found more than embarrassing. This was her profession. Her art. Nothing could shake her. Not a car backfiring on a street performance or a heckler at a show. Anything could happen, and she wouldn't move. Not even a fraction of a centimeter.

Not when gallery owner Patterson Simone got his throat slit in the front row, and not when that psycho kicked an old lady all the way down the aisle, taking a folding chair and smashing it against her temple until he got winded.

Nella didn't move a muscle.

Surrounded by a growing pile of dead bodies and under the gaze of a madman stalking the event space in NoHo, she thought, *yeah dad, this might just save my life.*

If she didn't move.

If she didn't speak.

If she could make it look like she wasn't breathing.

This evening's performance was a last-minute job offer. With the economy in shambles, Nella took any gig she could find. Tonight, a gallery opening for social media sensation Mar$ell da Champ at Caverna Bellezza in North Hollywood, celebrating his transition from iInternetnternet rapper she'd never heard of into artist that she'd never heard of. Two hours of mostly standing still, sometimes interacting with patrons when it made sense. Another hour of stillness while the main show took place. One more hour after that during reception, plus a photo op with Mar$ell to enhance her clout. Or something.

Easy gig.

She'd chosen The White Lady, one of her lazy looks, a costume mimicking a Roman maiden statue in an Elizabethan Garden. There were two maiden statues in the back of the gallery performance space, so she figured she'd blend in as the third. Stiff, voluminous layers of white fabric draped over a shiny spandex bodysuit that she'd painted to resemble smooth marble. She shellacked her hair, slicking it over her head, covering it with a wimple. She didn't want to bother with perfect hands, so she pulled on white nitrile gloves and added props, a basket of grapes in one hand, a bundle of flowers and vines in the other. At high-end openings, she'd sometimes go body painted, one breast bare to really nail the look, painting thin cracks and dark grey veins in faux marble on her skin. This job wasn't paying enough for that.

It *really* wasn't paying enough.

She'd arrived an hour early, hustling through final preparations in the women's bathroom. Most of the base layer of her face makeup was done at home, so it was a quick job to finish the look and practice a few facial expressions. She took some selfies, scrutinizing for giveaway areas, her eyes, the edges of her lips. She took great pride in her craft. She didn't want a hint of her dark skin to show through, no thin streaks in the paint. Anything visible to the human eye had to look like stone. She used a prosthetic nose that reshaped her face and covered her nostrils, simulating the dead-end carving you'd expect to see in a statue. Tiny screens lined the bottom edges, hidden very carefully, so she could still breathe through her nose. As long as she didn't breathe hard, it worked perfectly and silently.

Watching another patron pinned to the ground, a knife driven into his eye, deep slow breaths were hard to find, but she found them. Because she was a professional. A living statue. Being *anything* else at this moment could mean her life.

There was a moment of perfect calm she found when settling into her first pose. She started with a difficult one, just to challenge herself. Left arm high, holding up the vines, right arm cradling the grapes, head turned down to look at them. A dancing peasant girl. She ran scenarios in her head. What would it take to move her? What could a patron say? She loved perfectly timed movements, but they had to be organic. Moving for movement's sake was hack work. If someone asked where the appetizers were, she'd dip low with the grapes. If they asked where the bathroom was, maybe she'd extend the flowers in that direction.

If someone came in and announced that they'd roofied the gathering of twenty to thirty people, chained the doors shut, started killing people, she'd hold very, *very* still.

Preview nights were usually fun: a small select group of friends of the artist, often celebrities and their entourages. It usually made for some fun stories the next day. Tomorrow's story would be a doozy. Tonight was all social media influencers. She knew some of their names but had no idea why they were famous. They'd probably been paid an ungodly amount to be there, while her paycheck would barely cover the electric bill with enough left over for a burger.

The waiter arrived twenty minutes late to the festivities in ill-fitting clothes, but made up for it by keeping everyone's glass full. Always there with a refill, always encouraging people to drink up. He had an odd, manic energy. One of those squirrely guys she'd usually keep her eye on at parties. She spent so long watching him flit around the room that she didn't realize it had been almost thirty minutes since she changed poses. None of these overpaid zoomers seemed to notice her or care, so why work harder?

The patrons gradually found their seats thirty minutes before the main presentation started. Some yawning, some napping. Nella figured they were just there to get a selfie with Mar$ell and stay checked out the rest of the night.

Twenty minutes past scheduled showtime and nothing was happening. These shows always started late. Nella composed an email in her head to demand overtime for when this thing inevitably went long.

The waiter clapped his hands. "Tonight's experience will be one to remember. Mar$ell da Champ is running late, but let's have a round of applause for gallery owner Patterson Simone for this memorable, wonderful night."

A smattering of applause. Some in the audience lazily checked their phones. Patterson slurred "Who is this?" to his date.

"An ode to the trappings of capitalism!" the waiter said, his voice shuddering like an old car cold-starting in a Boston winter.

A waiter starting the evening with performance art wouldn't be the weirdest thing Nella had seen at a gig.

"We're breaking out of the prison of stale ideas tonight, but first, you need to understand how capitalism shackles you." The waiter lifted a table skirt in the corner and rolled out a small suitcase. He unzipped it as music played, dumping out a pile of handcuffs and chains. He ran a length of chain between the two door handles and padlocked it.

Nella had seen this kind of shitty agitprop art before, so she wasn't nervous as much as annoyed. Those were the only doors out of the space. The little prat better have a key ready if an emergency broke out. The waiter danced back to the stage, picking up a small stack of handcuffs, moving from patron to patron, locking wrist to chair, or ankle to chair, or letting some patrons cuff themselves to each other. Some laughed giddily, others groggily looked at their limp arms as he cuffed them. He collected every cell phone, gently placing them in a black velvet bag and announcing Mar$ell wanted this to be an exclusive experience. Phones would be returned after the show. Nella thought he didn't want any video evidence of how bad this performance might get.

She had the urge to comedically sit on the edge of her plinth, chin in hand, a bored-out-of-her-mind pose in protest of the pretention.

The waiter tore his shirt off and brandished a knife. "We're going to make a group painting inspired by Jackson Pollock, by Kandinsky, by Ed Gein and GG Allin." He drew the knife across his chest, bringing a cascade of blood, then clenched the handle between his thighs as he gyrated and thrusted lustily. He swept his palms over his chest, painting himself red.

He took a patron in the first row—Nella thought it might be Jin-Ae, the famous K-Pop singer, but she couldn't quite tell—placing his hands on her cheeks, pulling her head forward and trying to kiss her. She pushed him away, laughing a little and muttering *Get your corn syrup on someone else, you dumb fuck...*

So, he did, grabbing the man next to her by his manbun, angling his head back while continuing to thrust his hips. The knife poked at the man's arms and chest. Mr. Manbun swatted at him like a drunken grizzly, no effort, his limbs jelly. Then the show started.

The waiter grabbed the knife from between his legs and swung it at the man's face. It sounded like someone had dropped a book. The man's head snapped around, spraying blood across everyone to his right. A nightmare began in slow motion, some guests were alert enough to shout, but they were all sloppy and subdued. The waiter drew the knife back and rammed it into the man's eye, then used the handle to yank him out of his seat. Jin-Ae, handcuffed to him, plopped down and started screaming.

"Let's talk about art!" the waiter shouted, unbuttoning his pants. "This will be a collaborative work. Our Last Night on Earth."

Nella seized. Did he think she was a statue, or did he know the truth? Had she moved? Had she jumped? Had he seen her move earlier?

"Let's talk about *important* art. I'm so tired of hearing that phrase, so tired of hearing it from all of you when you buy shit like this," he gestured to the gallery, "while I'm on the Venice Boardwalk trying to make *ten fucking dollars* on prints."

He paused as if waiting for an answer. A few of the patrons drunkenly murmured *stop it, please* and *just leave, leave us alone* and one not-so-helpful *art is hard, I understand you.*

"I work *sixty-five-thousand dollars of student debt* hard. I work *shitty nine-to-five job to buy supplies and another seven-to-midnight job to buy food* hard. *Max out my credit cards to chase my dream* hard. *Can't even sell a print to friends or family* hard. And then I caught Patterson Simone's eye on the boardwalk. I finally got noticed. Felt like winning the lottery. I was down to my last hundred dollars and he blessed my work with his bony fingers and said I could get a gallery showing. Here. Tonight. And then, shit like this—"

The waiter stalked over to the wall and yanked a painting free. He cradled it, looked at it, an abstract of twin women on either side of an empty Instagram frame, one reaching through to get her hand kissed. "This one's good, actually."

He moved to another one, a small portrait of a girl with big eyes and bad skin staring at the viewer, challenging them to… *look*, Nella supposed.

The waiter yanked it off the wall and drove a fist through it, holding it by the sides. He jabbed it like a battering ram into the nearest patron's nose. Nella couldn't tell if the crack she heard was the frame, or the man's nose, or both.

"Four nights ago, I called to make final preparations and I was told about a schedule mix-up. Another event had been previously scheduled which they *just discovered*, Jesus Christ, Patterson, we all have social media. We all saw the posts about the surprise show from Mar$ell da Champ. You didn't have to lie to me. I spent months putting every spare penny into supplies and new works. Prints to sell. I can't wait until *a later date* because I won't have food to get me there. You backlisted me in favor of a social media dimwit. I was promised a showing tonight, and I will have it!"

Patterson slurred *I never*— as the waiter lifted the broken frame over his head, slamming it down over the patron's broken nose. He moved behind the man, putting a foot on his chair and wrapping the remnants of the frame around the man's neck, pulling back hard.

A chorus of slurred screams arose. The patron made noises from his nose and mouth and chest that Nella had never heard. And she didn't move. Didn't blink. Only wished he'd have attacked someone outside of her peripheral vision. She wanted to take her mind somewhere else, the same way she would when some asshole on the street tried to lift her skirt. Everything but sexual harassment could be weathered, because other passers-by usually saw it and broke it up and left bigger tips.

Why isn't he dying? Why does it take so long to choke someone to death?

Get out of the moment. Go somewhere else. This can be endured. Think of school, student debt, Dad's rejection, Mom not being alive to see the aftermath of whatever happened tonight.

Go somewhere else. Don't go out of body, stay in the art. Art saved her soul. There was no failure in art. There was no success. There was only communication. Before communication to an audience, there was communication to self, opening to self, loving *self*, and that was a breakthrough. Maybe there'd never be money, but there'd always be time. That's what her therapist told her, her stupid therapist who wasn't here to see this, her therapist who should tell that maniac about self-love or time or money and she can't focus on anything but *here and now*, which is what her therapist would want, but not in this sense, not because the waiter just pulled another knife from his belt.

He moved between rows, rubbing a hand across his still-bleeding chest and slapping patrons. He grabbed a hunk of a woman's shirt and sliced it off, holding it above his head. "These stains aren't ever coming out. You're gonna remember this night forever. And hey, speaking of laundering, that's all these things are really, right? Just a big fuckin' tax dodge. You're either here to launder money by paying way too much for shit, or you're here for selfies and *look-at-me* social media bullshit. Right?"

He picked up a bottle of wine from the serving station in the corner, flipping it over, brandishing the bulbous bottle like a club. He pointed at a man in the second row. "You're the guy that paid two hundred and fifty K for Silvio Gueta's *Folded Cardboard*, right? Some shit-for-brains hack saves his boxes from Amazon and glues them together into... what the fuck was it supposed to be? What was it supposed to *be*?" He slammed the bottle across the man's head.

Nella only heard the symphony of violence: the hollow melon *pop*, the slight *crunch*, a weird liquid *bloop*, and the dying cow noise the man made. Nella thought she'd hear it every night when she closed her eyes. If she got out of here.

The man hit the floor face first, shoulders and knees down, ass pointing toward the sky. His right ankle was cuffed to his chair, turned at an impossibly sharp angle. The way he twitched and huffed, he was probably on his way to a place where he wouldn't have to worry about feeling the pain of that broken joint.

The waiter looked at the bottle, coated in a slick of blood. "I thought it would break, didn't you?" He stalked to the front of the theater. Nella took the opportunity to scan the room, looking for any way out. One set of swinging doors, chained closed. No windows, because this was a performance space. No weapons she could get to that he couldn't get to first. A fire alarm on the wall by the door. She might be able to reach it, but then what? She'd get stabbed or beaten under flashing lights and sirens and a cascade of water. If she ran full-tilt at the door, the chain might not break, but maybe the handles would snap, maybe the frame would crack. How fast could she run wearing forty pounds of shellacked fabric and crinoline?

Sirens outside. Growing louder. *Hallelujah! could this be*— but they passed. This was North Hollywood after dark. Ambulances always hauled ass down Lankershim. So did cops. Nobody was coming.

"I had sixty dollars to my name. I thought I'd be spending it tonight to celebrate my grand opening while I waited for all of the money from sales to come in. I wanted everyone to leave here tonight smiling, texting their friends to see if they knew anything about Willem Ellis Foster, the amazing new artist. Wunderkind. The forty-six-year-old wunderkind." Foster's lower lip trembled and his shoulders sagged.

Nella shuddered. She knew the name from social media. Someone had shared a photo of his booth on the Venice Boardwalk with a snarky caption. Foster had painted a large placard to hang behind his works with the hashtag #WEFart. Nella had a hard time piling on when people made fun of struggling artists. Existing, waking up, that was enough of a kick in the nuts every day. But a hashtag that could be misconstrued as *we fart?* Her diaphragm bucked, the corner of her mouth twitched. This was not the time for laughter. It was going to happen. Push it down. Think of something else.

"I gave it all I had."

#WEFart. *Don't laugh.*

"You pulled this out of me."

We. Fart. Why now?

"I have nothing left to give." Foster slaps his stomach, then his heart. "I'm emptied out."

Nella crossed big toe over middle, subtly shifting her weight until it felt like her toe might pop, sprain, snap. Pain. Make it hurt, because none of this was funny. Not that stupid look on his face. Not some stupid fart joke.

Foster moved to the refreshment station. "I know some really good drug dealers. Sixty dollars to the right dude will get you a big-ass bag of bennies. Wine and Benzodiazepine. Half of you probably use this as your normal nightcap. Gives you kind of a warm and happy buzz, right? I mean… Can I make you happy? Where are *you* going?"

A woman in her fifties—or maybe later, LA had some good surgeons—crawled toward the swinging doors. "You trying to leave? You want a souvenir?" Foster reared back and kicked her in the ass, hard enough that she skidded forward and folded up. He kept kicking until she started crawling again. Closer and closer to Nella's plinth. "We're all taking a different way out tonight." Foster grabbed an empty folding chair, hoisting it and slamming one leg into the woman's temple. He kept driving, down, down, down, down, until she stopped moving.

Nella heard the blood patter against her plinth. A shard of the woman's veneers shattered and ejected with such force that they hit the statue next to her. That pebble-tic noise. Louder than a bullet. Foster's naked torso was covered in a sheen of pink blood-sweat that washed into obscure patterns across the waist of his khakis.

Don't see me. I am not real. I am not real.

He stood in front of Nella, staring down at the dead woman, panting, heaving, then arching his neck and head back to let out a primal scream.

"I don't know what I'm doing! I'm sorry. I'm sorry, can you forgive me? Can you… can I have a…?"

Foster grabbed the leg of the statue to Nella's left, just outside of her peripheral vision. She had no way to brace for what might happen next. His hand slapped at the marble or plaster or whatever it was made of. Then he caressed it. Rubbed it. Through the plasticine folds of her dress, she felt heat rising off his body. His scent was electric, animal, frightening. He slapped the neighboring statue's legs and moved before Nella, head down, hair slick with sweat and blood. Through lowered eyelids she studied his blotchy red back, two pimples on one shoulder, a bald patch starting to form on his crown, stray curls of hair growing wild on the sides of his neck.

He put his palms on either side of her dress. Did he hear her heart pounding? Feel it hammering down through her legs into the plinth? Were her shaking knees making everything vibrate?

He slowly tilted his head back, back, back…

The doors heaved. Someone yanked them, making the chains pop and rattle. From outside, "Hello?"

Silence.

Foster's wild eyes took in the room, begging someone to tell him what to do next.

"Yo! Is this the right room? Did you bring me to the wrong place, you little bitch?" This, followed by some light giggles. Mar$ell and his PA. A muffled conversation. The drugged patrons started to moan. Someone yelled for help, but it sounded like the moan of an old person with a bad back sitting down after a long day of work.

"Is someone fucking in there?"

"You are so bad! This is the place. I don't know…"

The doors rattled again, three big bounding swings, until a gap appeared between the doors wide enough for someone to peek through.

"Mar$ell is here, bitches! Open up and love me!"

Foster moved away from Nella's plinth. Cold relief poured down her spine. Sweat trickled down her thighs inside the cocoon of her dress, maybe a little pee, too. Her spine stiffened as Foster moved toward the door.

"Shhhh, shhh, shhh." Foster walked theatrically, picking his knees up high and gingerly stepping over sprawled bodies. He spun and pounced on Jin-Ae's date in the front row, the man with the knife stuck in his head. He planted a foot on his skull and yanked the knife free. "Shhhhhhh…We're going to surprise him!"

He grabbed the padlock as he raised his voice. "Ladies and gentlemen, it's time to welcome the guest of honor, acclaimed artist and activist, Mar$ell da Champ!" Foster pulled the chain free from the handles and kicked the doors open, bringing a yelp of surprise from the hallway.

Foster rushed through the doors and out of Nella's vision. This was her only chance. Maybe he was chasing Mar$ell into the street. He might not notice if she ran. Might see the woman clumsily scrambling in her forty-pound dress (maybe fifty soaked with sweat) and decide she wasn't worth it. Nella grabbed the sides of her dress, tensed her knees.

A slap from the hallway, a scream, footsteps, and then Mar$ell da Champ flew through the doors, blood blossoming across his white turtleneck and white pants. Nella snapped back into her pose, hoping Foster wouldn't notice any slight changes in her dress, her hands, her eyes.

Mar$ell, alabaster white, in his faux hip-hop colonizer I'm-so-deep-and-so-grounded apparel, scooted on his butt, unsure of which way to go. "Call the cops!" he shouted down the hallway.

Foster smiled, a man close to finding peace.

Mar$ell pressed a hand to his shredded shirt, fingering the deep gash running below his collarbone. He wore a shiny white porcelain replica of a chain link necklace, white belt on white pants that were thousand-dollar replicas of things Nella saw at the swap meet every weekend. White Adidas, white socks. Everything white. So white. But turning pink, turning red.

"You're everything that's wrong with the world, Mar-*sellout!* The only people who like you are idiots who only like things that richer, smarter idiots like, because they want to fit in. And the rich, smart idiots only talk about work from real artists because they want to seem *relatable.* The snake is eating its tail! Nobody outside of this room really cares who you are, but I'm gonna make you a household name!" Foster paced like a caged animal between a toppled chair and a corked wine bottle. He flipped the knife over and over, head shaking side-to-side like an invisible hand was slapping him.

He grew still. Deflated. "You're still gonna win. This is just going to make you more money. No matter what. You're just going to use this to... oh shit." Foster swiped a tear from his face and sat, pale belly wrinkling. "I messed up. I messed it up. Can you say you're sorry? Can you just tell me you're sorry for stealing my big opening?"

Patterson Simone slapped at the floor. "I don't know who you are. I don't know how you got the idea that—" while Mar$ell said, "I didn't... I'm not..." He sounded like a scared college kid.

"You did. You did!" Foster pounced from the chair, driving his knife into Mar$ell's thigh. He rolled away, leaving Mar$ell screaming and clutching at the handle. "I can't. All I wanted to do at this… I have a bit of a temper. I know. I should be in therapy. That was another thing I was going to look into with my money from tonight…" Foster stalked away, then leapt and stomped his foot down onto the knife handle. Mar$ell screamed and curled into a ball, crying. "And you're here buying stupid gold teeth, stupid, fake…" Foster pinned Mar$ell's head against the floor with one hand and rested the cork of the bottle against his lips. "Smile. Smile, motherfucker, show me those teeth, I'm gonna break 'em. Gonna take 'em home with me…"

Nella looked from his heaving back to the open door. Twenty feet away. He was preoccupied.

Foster bucked his weight onto the bottle. Mar$ell cried out in pain as the bottle bounced off his teeth and scraped down his face. Foster stood and dropped the bottle on Mar$ell's nose. "Fuck, I'm exhausted! Now I know why people do mass shootings…" He laughed. Hard. Doubled over, tears streaming down his cheeks. His lower jaw was rigor-mortis straight, lower teeth exposed. A bubble of snot expanded and contracted in his right nostril. His eyes darted around the room, settling on Nella.

Sirens outside. Growing louder. Layering. Stopping. Ambulance? Police? Why couldn't Nella remember the difference in siren sounds?

Foster grabbed Mar$ell's collar, dragging him to Patterson Simone's side. Patterson touched Mar$ell's leg. Foster stamped down, crunching fingers and wrist, then drew himself up, picking up the bloody wine bottle from the floor. "That's what it feels like to get your thunder stolen. We're equals. Who wants top billing with me on the morning news? High-society Patterson Simone or trust fund baby Mar$ell da Champ? Should we leave it up to the fates?"

Foster walked to the back of the room, standing before the three statues. Nella held her breath. Was she sweating? Could he see it? Did he smell her? She prayed the itch on her cheek was just a nervous tic and not her prosthetic nose coming loose.

Trust the art.

Don't move. Never move.

"Which one are you?" Foster asked her. "What are these?" he spun to the room. "Are these the Fates? This doesn't look Greek, what are they supposed to—whose work is this?" Foster ran a finger along one of the folded ridges in Nella's dress, confusion registering on his brow. He grabbed it and wiggled it.

A distant thud in the hallway. The rustle of nylon and squeak of leather and rubber that had to be police boots, had to be a gunbelt, *dear God, please…*

"Which one do I take?" he asked her, then repeated the question to the other statues.

Echoing down the hall, "LAPD!"

The patrons who hadn't passed out murmured and moaned.

"They're not talking…" Foster locked eyes with Nella. "Which one? Which one, tell me."

Nella was certain she'd been discovered. Foster was out of time. He charged toward Patterson and Mar$ell, raising his knife. Patterson lifted his arm feebly, but Foster swatted it aside, grabbing him by his tiny ponytail and yanking his head back. He looked at Nella again. "Is one enough? Will they remember me?"

He drew his blade across Patterson's throat, a cascade of blood spraying across the crowd. A drop of something warm and wet hit Nella's chin.

Sweat. Just sweat. Don't move.

Foster grabbed the bottle from the floor and clubbed it across Mar$ell's head. The artist went limp. Foster, amazed that the bottle still hadn't broken, walked out of the room trying to open it. He paused in front of Nella, working the cork, his eyes never leaving hers.

The cork came free and the bottle slipped from his hands, smashing on the floor. He looked up at her from the dark puddle, two clean tracks of tears washing blood from his cheeks. "Shhhh."

Foster walked out of the room. What the hell had the cops been waiting for? Down the hall, a door opened and closed. Muffled voices. Did they let him walk out? Had he escaped?

Still, Nella didn't move. Now she had her own private showing of a tableau vivant, Pieter Bruegel the Elder's *Triumph of Death*. The patrons, those left alive, arms and legs swimming drug-sloppy-slow in the air while others slowly bled out. Nella watched it unfold, convinced if she moved or made a sound, Foster would return to kill her. Had he known the whole time, or was he a madman barking at a statue?

A policeman walked in, followed by another. Then some paramedics. Nella focused on their guns, their batons, handcuffs. She did not move.

Did they get him? Was he free?

She stayed motionless on the plinth until all of the victims were carted out. Even when they taped off the room to contain the crime scene. Even when they turned out the lights. She wouldn't talk. She wouldn't move. She wouldn't make a sound. Alone in her art, on a pedestal, she was safe. She was alive. This was her world. It would be days until she could make a sound. Maybe weeks. Maybe forever.

Trust the art. The art was all she had, everything in the world.

AUTHOR BIOGRAPHIES

Editor bio:

Ken MacGregor writes stuff. Sometimes, he edits stuff too.

He has two story collections: AN ABERRANT MIND, and SEX, GORE & MILLIPEDES, a young adult novella: DEVIL'S BANE, a co-written (with Kerry Lipp), novel: HEADCASE (available in serialized form), and is a member of the Great Lakes Association of Horror Writers (GLAHW). He is a somewhat regular contributor to HorrorTree with his column *Brain Babies*. He has also written TV commercials, sketch comedy, a music video, some mediocre poetry, and a zombie movie. Ken is the Managing Editor of Collections and Anthologies for LVP Publications. Prior to this one, he curated an anthology: BURNT FUR for Blood Bound Books.

When not writing, Ken drives the bookmobile for his local library. He lives with his kids, two cats, and the ashes of his wife.

Ken can be found at ken-macgregor.com. You can also connect with him via social media on the following platforms:

- Twitter: @kenmacgregor
- Facebook:https://www.facebook.com/KenMacGregorAuthor
- Pinterest: https://www.pinterest.com/macgregorken/

Author bios:

RL Meza:

R. L. Meza lives in a century-old Victorian house on the coast of northern California with her husband and the host of strange animals that she calls family. When she isn't writing horror stories, roaming through the forest, or painting fungi, she can be found with a cat in her lap and a book in her hand.

Sarah Hans:

Sarah Hans is an award-winning writer, editor, and teacher whose stories have appeared in more than 30 publications, including *The Arcanist* and *Pseudopod*. Her first dark fantasy novel, ENTOMOPHOBIA, is scheduled to be published in Spring of 2021 by Omnium Gatherum. You can read more of Sarah's short stories in the collection DEAD GIRLS DON'T LOVE, published by Dragon's Roost Press, or by backing her Patreon for just $1. You can also find her on twitter under the handle @steampunkpanda.

Linda Nagle:

An editor of over twenty years, Linda also writes her own weird brand of shite that nobody understands aside from all both of her readers. Wildly unpopular with lovers of excessive eyebrow references and terrible sex scenes, she has a penchant for swearing and silliness, although she has been known to get serious at times (GREAT BRITISH HORROR, Vol. 5 —Black Shuck Books) and downright disgusting at others (*Splatterpunk Zine* —Sinister Horror Company). She uses her alter ego for that shit—CM Franklyn has no filter. You can also find her ramblings in a bunch of anthologies whose makers were bonkers enough to publish them (Chinbeard Books, Haverhill House, Burdizzo Books, I'm looking at you!). The zombie story she said she'd never write appears in NIGHT OF THE LIVING CURE (Wolfgang Anthologies), and you can find "Beware of the Bull," the story that fragile white men despise, at liberatetutemet.com. Her debut collection, STRANGER COMPANIES (Kuboa Press), is now out of print, so there is no point having mentioned it here. A bunch of equally experimental wordage is forthcoming, but for now, you can rest easy in the knowledge that she has four kids, two cats, and a pair of breasts she already knows about (without the need for surprise boobal exposition via mirror breaks and/or shower scenes of a revelatory nature). Oh—and she once killed Ken MacGregor. Sort of.

Lucy A. Snyder:

Lucy A. Snyder is the Shirley Jackson Award-nominated and five-time Bram Stoker Award-winning author of 14 books and over 100 published short stories. Her most recent books are the collection HALLOWEEN SEASON and the forthcoming novel THE GIRL WITH THE STAR-STAINED SOUL. Her writing has appeared in publications such as *Asimov's Science Fiction, Apex Magazine, Nightmare Magazine, Pseudopod, Fireside Quarterly, Strange Horizons,* and *Best Horror of the Year.* She lives in Columbus, Ohio. You can learn more about her at www.lucysnyder.com and you can follow her on Twitter at @LucyASnyder.

Lee Murray:

Lee Murray is a multi-award-winning writer and editor of science fiction, fantasy, and horror (Sir Julius Vogel, Australian Shadows) and a three-time Bram Stoker Award® nominee. Her works include the Taine McKenna military thrillers, and supernatural crime-noir series The Path of Ra co-written with Dan Rabarts, debut collection GROTESQUE: MONSTER STORIES, and several books for children. She is the editor of sixteen anthologies, the most recent being BLACK CRANES: TALES OF UNQUIET WOMEN (with Geneve Flynn), and the AHWA's MIDNIGHT ECHO #15. She is co-founder of Young New Zealand Writers and of the Wright-Murray Residency for Speculative Fiction Writers, and is HWA Mentor of the Year for 2019 and an Honorary Literary Fellow of the New Zealand Society of Authors. Lee lives in New Zealand's sunny Bay of Plenty where she dreams up stories from her office overlooking a cow paddock. Read more at www.leemurray.info @leemurraywriter

ZZ Claybourne:

Zig Zag Claybourne is the author of THE BROTHERS JETSTREAM: LEVIATHAN and its sequel AFRO PUFFS ARE THE ANTENNAE OF THE UNIVERSE. Other novels include BY ALL

OUR VIOLENT GUIDES and NEON LIGHTS. His stories and essays on sci fi, fandom, and life have appeared in *Apex*, *Galaxy's Edge*, *GigaNotosaurus*, *Strange Horizons*, and other genre venues, as well as the "42" blog at www.writeonrighton.com. He grew up watching *The Twilight Zone* and considers himself a better person for it.

Joanna Koch:

Joanna Koch writes literary horror and surrealist trash. Author of THE COUVADE and THE WINGSPAN OF SEVERED HANDS, Joanna is a Shirley Jackson award finalist whose short fiction can be found in Year's Best Hardcore Horror 5, Not All Monsters, and The Big Book of Blasphemy. Find Joanna at horrorsong.blog and on Twitter @horrorsong.

Gabino Iglesias:

Gabino Iglesias is a writer, editor, professor, and book critic living in Austin, TX. He is the author of ZERO SAINTS and COYOTE SONGS and the editor of BOTH SIDES. His work has been nominated to the Bram Stoker and Locus awards and won the Wonderland Book Award for Best Novel. His nonfiction has appeared in the *New York Times* and the *Los Angeles Times*. His fiction has been published in five languages and optioned for film. His reviews appear in places like NPR, *Publishers Weekly*, *the San Francisco Chronicle*, *Criminal Element*, *Mystery Tribune*, *Vol. 1 Brooklyn*, *the Los Angeles Review of Books*, and other venues. He's been a juror for the Shirley Jackson Awards twice and has judged the PANK Big Book Contest, the Splatterpunk Awards, the horror category of the British Fantasy Awards, and the Newfound Prose Prize. He teaches creative writing at Southern New Hampshire University's online MFA program and runs a series of low-cost online writing workshops. You can find him on Twitter at @Gabino_Iglesias

Hailey Piper:

Hailey Piper is the author of THE WORM AND HIS KINGS, BENNY ROSE, THE CANNIBAL KING, and THE POSSESSION OF NATALE GLASGOW. She is a member of the

HWA, and her short fiction appears in YEAR'S BEST HARDCORE HORROR, *Flash Fiction Online*, *The Arcanist*, and elsewhere. A trans woman from the haunted woods of New York, she now lives with her wife in Maryland, where they spend weekends raising the dead. Find Hailey at www.haileypiper.com and on Twitter via @HaileyPiperSays.

Patty Templeton:

Patty Templeton is a writer, archivist, artist, and itinerant kitchen dancer. She has a MSLIS with an archival focus from the University of Illinois at Urbana-Champaign, is a 2020 Library of Congress Junior Fellow, and is a provisional member of the Academy of Certified Archivists.

She is the author of the historical fantasy novel THERE IS NO LOVELY END, an 1880s ghost story following the life of rifle heiress Sarah Winchester. Currently she's writing a novel in stories about a small city in perpetual autumn. Templeton enjoys hot coffee, loud rock shows, and reading while wrapped in rhinestones. She'd be grateful if you checked out PrisonBookProgram.org/PrisonBookNetwork to see how you can help incarcerated folks receive free books.

Michael Paul Gonzalez:

Michael Paul Gonzalez is the author of the novels ANGEL FALLS and MISS MASSACRE'S GUIDE TO MURDER AND VENGEANCE and the short story collection CARRY ME HOME: STORIES OF HORROR AND HEARTBREAK. He wrote and produced the serial horror audio drama LARKSPUR UNDERGROUND, available for free on iTunes and Stitcher. An active member of the Horror Writers Association, his short stories have appeared in print and online, including Lost Signals, Gothic Fantasy: Chilling Horror Stories, the Booked. Podcast Anthology, Tales from the Crust: A Pizza Horror Anthology, HeavyMetal.com, and the Appalachian Undead Anthology. He resides in Los Angeles, a place full of wonders and monsters far stranger than any that live in the imagination. You can visit him online at MichaelPaulGonzalez.com

DRAGON'S ROOST PRESS

Dragon's Roost Press is the fever dream brainchild of dark speculative fiction author Michael Cieslak. Since 2014, their goal has been to find the best speculative fiction authors and share their work with the public. For more information about Dragon's Roost Press and their publications, please visit: https://thedragonsroost.biz

facebook.com/DragonsRoostPress

twitter.com/thedragonsroost

Made in the USA
Monee, IL
17 April 2022

94466465R00089